Are you craving a little sunshine and adventure?
Whether you have an exotic holiday of a lifetime
booked, are looking forward to a staycation,
or even planning some armchair travel, you're
going to need some top quality fiction
by your side.
For Little Escapes Around the World, the second
book in our Little Escapes series, we delved into
the My Weekly fiction archives to find a wonderful
collection of stories to transport you to some of
the most beautiful corners of the globe.
This fabulous collection of short stories from some
of our best-loved writers, includes everything from
a budding new romance in sun-kissed Corfu to a
wonderful Spanish adventure in Alicante.
From comforting tales of female friendship to
inspiring road trips with a touch of romance,
we hope you enjoy your literary trip.
Pour yourself a pina colada, find a sunny spot
and enjoy!

**Susan Watson,
Commissioning
Fiction Editor,
My Weekly magazine**

D0307782

CONTENTS

A Brush With Greece

April and her daughter Libby finally find the space to relax and find their inner selves

By MANDY BAGGOTT

I t's cracked... in three places!"

At first during that phone call two weeks ago, April thought her friend, Carole, was telling her about another dishwasher mishap. But on this occasion Carole hadn't been talking about a ruined cereal bowl, but a broken right arm.

"I was so looking forward to all that fragrant sea air, blue skies and the hope that Nikos would turn naked life model instead of teacher..." Carole had let out a sigh at the end of the sentence that told April her friend's much-looked-forward-to art retreat on the Greek island of Corfu might not have been just about the watercolours.

So, one forty-something single woman's loss was another forty-something divorcee's gain. On Carole's bossy insistence, with the threat of being whacked with her new plaster cast, April had accepted her friend's place on the course as long as her daughter, fifteen-year-old Libby, could go too.

And now here they were. Corfu, Greece. Halfway up a mountain, the humidity rising almost as quickly as Libby's angst, the car stopped and unable to proceed further due to the fixed position of an angry-looking goat.

"Mum! Do something!"

April was outside the car, cautiously considering action while Libby literally cowered in the back seat, windows closed, hoodie pulled over her head, iPhone gripped in her hand, eyes darting around as if the

intransigent goat might attack at any moment.

The goat gave a snort and stamped a hoof as April took a step towards it. It reminded her a little of a grumpy bull getting riled by a matador. The difference was, they were in Greece, not Spain, and April had neither a red cape to defend herself nor any sun cream on her arms yet.

"Mum!" Libby shouted. "Shut the car door! A bee might fly in!"

April wavered, caught between turning back to the car or continuing her advance on the wiry black-and-white animal, now losing steam from its nostrils. Right now, she didn't want to be here.

Why had she agreed to this? An artists' retreat! The only "art" she attempted nowadays was a short back and sides of the garden hedge, now she had sole responsibility for it. Libby and a pair of shears didn't bear thinking about. That chore shared would likely end up with a trip to A&E.

"Now, you listen to me," April addressed the goat, blowing her fringe off her forehead and planting her sandal-covered feet down in an attempt at dominance. "You move out of our way, just a little bit, and then you can have the whole track to yourself forever for all I care!" ➤

"Mum! The bees!" Libby shouted again.

With sweat trickling down the side of her face, the midday sun an oppressive greenhouse hot, April lunged forward, zapping her hands backwards and forwards, then side to side, in a cross between karate and desperate-hailing-of-a-cab-in-London. This was the very first break she and Libby had had since the divorce was finalised at Christmas and she wasn't going to let a farmyard animal ruin it.

"Shoo!" April ordered, dust flying up into the air as she turned all bad-attitude and stomped her authority over the Greek road. "Shoo!"

With one final kung-fu kick that April was sure Libby would be cringing over the sight of if she wasn't so worried about flying insects, the goat gave a low rumble of a disgruntled growl and finally trotted off into the bushes.

Mission accomplished! And April couldn't deny it felt good. She'd won a battle with a local beast, now it was time to see if she could master an easel and a paintbrush.

"Mum! I don't like it here!"

April drew in an edifying breath, taking a little time to really see the scenery surrounding her. Yes, she might currently be melting like Boris Johnson during a tough Prime Minister's Questions session, but this piece of Greek paradise all around was picture-perfect.

Spiralling down from the rough mountainside track were undulating peaks and troughs filled with olive and cypress trees, bright and beautiful wildflowers in pinks and yellows and white, ending in a climax that was a glistening azure sea.

Libby wasn't a fan of any kind of change and the teenager had been through quite enough since John had packed his golf clubs and taken a tiny piece of his daughter's broken heart with him to Scotland. But perhaps this unseen "break" and the Greek way of life for a week would be good for them both.

Villa Kitrinos looked like the house the TV Durrell family inhabited. Thick rustic stone, hundreds of years old, with beamed ceilings and pink marble floors. It had been a former home of monks – and it was almost as imposing as it was welcoming.

And April and Libby had been welcomed wholeheartedly from the very moment their hire car had pulled to a jerky halt outside and Libby had flung open the door, running from the absolute certainty that a wasp had invaded the car's interior.

Nikos. April sighed then, allowing her brush to linger a little too long on the canvas set on her easel. Villa Kitrinos and its artist owner were both exactly how the website depicted them.

Nikos was all black hair and dark eyes, with a tall, athletic frame had caught Libby as she circled round and round, flapping and fanning and swatting away imaginary bugs as four other guests all looked up from their paintings curious about the new arrivals.

This piece of Greek paradise all around was picture perfect

April had immediately bristled, knowing how little Libby cared for physical contact – even from her – and she'd waited for the severe reaction she was sure would be forthcoming. But strangely there hadn't been any reaction of that sort at all. Instead Nikos had whirled her around and around in his arms speaking funny words in his native tongue. Libby had laughed, her feet finally coming to a rest on the cobbled terrace when Nikos put her down.

That had been five days ago now and April had enjoyed each and every long deliciously sunny hour of every day being somewhere other than Surrey. Here, in the village of Loutses, it was like the rest of the world and all its stresses had simply fallen away amid the olive and almond trees.

"Mum," Libby whispered. "Do you think Nikos would give us the recipe for the sofrito he made last night so that we can make it when we get home?"

April's heart swelled at her teenager's words. Libby was strictly a three-cheese pizza kind of a girl who considered cauliflower an exotic vegetable. For her to request the rich, garlic-infused veal dish was ➔

real progress. This had to be Corfu – the slow, soft pace of life, the cicadas' song, the deeply flavoured gastronomy – seeping under their skin and reviving them both.

"I think you should definitely ask him," April replied. "It was so delicious, wasn't it?"

But not quite as delicious as Nikos himself. April's skin suddenly woke up as she recalled the previous night. Under a starlit sky, Nikos had given April a tour of the grounds around Villa Kitrinos. There was half-an-acre filled with gnarled olive trees, wild asparagus and figs, the view of the sea an evermoving backdrop of pure serenity.

This tree has not just beauty, but inner strength and resilience

Nikos had held her hand like it was the most natural thing in the world to clasp the fingers of someone he had known only five days. And, as April looked into those dark sultry eyes, she let herself wallow in this attention.

She wasn't naïve enough to think that Nikos had put this moonlit ramble on for her alone this summer, but that didn't matter. What mattered was that April allowed herself to move with it, accept it was a beginning of her new chapter. She was no longer John's wife and golf widow, she was April Radley, spending August on a Greek island with her daughter, and loving every second of connecting paintbrush to paper – and imagining connecting her lips to a Greek Adonis...

"Ooo, Mum, there's a tortoise!"

Libby was off her stool, trotting to discover the kind of wildlife she could appreciate without the worry of being bitten or stung. Her daughter was already brighter and more confident than April had seen in so long.

"You have chosen to paint my very favourite olive tree."

It was Nikos's deep accented voice close to her ear and already April could feel the goose bumps spreading over her lightly tanned skin. She smiled, regarding her definitely-getting-better attempt on her easel.

"Oh, Nikos," she replied, looking up at him. "There are so many beautiful trees in your garden. How can you possibly have a favourite?"

He smiled at her, dark hair falling over his face, as he dipped his head a little lower into her space. "This tree," he began in no more than a whisper. "This tree does not know of its beauty." He brought an olive-skinned finger to April's canvas, running his pad over the outline of her painting. It was all April could do not to wonder what those long deft fingers might feel like grazing the outline of her naked body...

"This tree," Nikos continued. "Its beauty is not just on the outside. It has inner strength and resilience. And a heart that is generous."

Suddenly April knew neither of them were talking about trees. Perhaps she could let herself, just for a moment, pretend she was twenty-four and not forty-four. Maybe she could lean in close to Nikos, breathe in his aroma of sunshine, sea salt and sculpting clay and see what would transpire next...

"Nikos, old chap, could you have a gander at my fine lines over here if it's not too much bother."

Major Faulkner – one of the other guests at Villa Kitrinos – had burst the romantic bubble and April sat up a little straighter on her stool. Nikos squeezed her shoulder as he left her – his touch firm and warm with a hint of a promise to revisit the moment.

Who was this April Farley sitting outside an ancient house in a gorgeous Greek village, her hair sun-kissed, her skin rich with vitamin D – and no bra? She didn't quite know this new version of her intimately yet, but she was beginning to like the very first blooms.

April's eyes went to the garden then, the wildflowers being tickled by a welcome breeze, the sea waving a greeting, and there was her Libby, strolling side-by-side with her new friend the wild tortoise. Letting out a contented sigh, April felt her shoulders relax even more fully. Perhaps this brush with Greece wasn't where their Corfu adventure was going to end. Maybe this summer was only the very beginning. ⓂⓌ

Malaysian Magic

Helen just wanted her daughter to be happy – and found happiness for herself, too

By JAN SNOOK

Helen walked out onto the balcony of her daughter's flat and breathed in the warm Malaysian air. The sun was dazzling, and she looked down at the gardens below, which were lush with banana plants, passion flowers, bougainvillaea, hibiscus and exotic plants that Helen didn't recognise. Golden Orioles flitted from tree to tree, and somewhere frogs were croaking. In the far distance the iconic Petronas Towers were glinting in the sun.

"Oh, you've woken up then? I thought you might still be suffering from jet lag."

Helen's daughter Lizzie had joined her on the balcony and was holding out a welcome cup of tea.

"I thought we'd go to the orchid park this morning. Orchids really grow like weeds out here. Of course they might make you cross," Lizzie added, her eyes laughing, "They're absolutely beautiful, and they're dirt cheap, nothing like the prices you pay in the UK!"

Helen smiled. "I'd like to go and see them all the same." Her face clouded. "Your father did love his orchids."

Lizzie squeezed her arm, and Helen gave a wan smile.

"Most of the time I'm fine. Really, I am," she added, seeing the doubt in her daughter's eyes. "Your father's orchids are still doing well. I honestly thought I was bound to kill them off after he died, but it's been three years and they're still thriving. They just don't look like the orchids here… The airport was awash with them! But are you sure you've got

time to do things with me today? Shouldn't you be at work?"

"Well, I wasn't going to abandon you the minute you arrived," Lizzie said, "And I do get holidays, you know. I will have to go to the office some of the time, I'm afraid, but once I've shown you where the shops are you'll be fine, won't you?"

"Of course I will. I've got my Kindle with me, absolutely loaded with books I want to read, and I intend on sitting by that gorgeous pool for hours on end."

The pool was on the roof, and offered even better views of Kuala Lumpur than from this balcony, Helen reflected.

"Well good," Lizzie said. "When I first got here I went for a swim every day, but after a while you get so used to having it that you don't use it. And at weekends I'm quite often in Redang, diving. In fact hardly anyone uses the pool – you'll have it to yourself."

Which would be just as well, Helen thought. She hadn't been seen in public in a swimming costume for quite a while, and she wasn't sure the public was ready for it.

"So you're still diving, then?" Helen enquired. "It must be a bit different diving here – not like Swanage."

Lizzie laughed. "You could say that. The fish are wonderful, and there are so many islands you're spoilt for choice." ➤

"And you do all this with… friends?" Helen asked, even though she had promised herself she wouldn't pry. Not, of course, that this was prying, she corrected herself hurriedly. You are allowed to ask your own daughter a few questions, aren't you? But she transferred her gaze from the view back to her daughter and was met with an amused silence.

"Well your emails aren't very informative," Helen said, half apologetic, half accusing. "I worry about you, being out here all alone."

"I can assure you that I don't spend much time 'all alone'," Lizzie said. "And yes, I go diving with friends most weekends. But not while you're here, obviously," she added quickly.

"And do you go in a… large group?"

"Mum! Yes! There are usually about half a dozen of us, but not everyone goes every weekend, OK? And if you really want to know, there are two couples, and six or seven singletons. Including one gorgeous man, who concentrates on his diving, and isn't remotely interested in me. OK, satisfied?"

Helen said nothing, but smiled expectantly.

"And his name's Tom, OK? That's it. All you're getting!"

The orchid park was certainly beautiful, as was the bird park which they visited the following afternoon. Huge gaudy hornbills and toucans swept overhead, while green peacocks strutted around the visitors, unconcerned.

It was a particularly hot day, and at four o'clock Helen and Lizzie stopped for a glass of iced tea at The Coffee Bean which was quite close to Lizzie's flat. Lizzie's mobile rang and she glanced at the screen and frowned.

"I ought to take this, sorry…" She got up and walked a short distance away, and Helen sat sipping her drink, fanning herself and covertly watching her daughter.

She could read her like a book, Helen thought. Her face when she'd seen who was calling had registered shock, then something very like hope, and now… now she looked anguished. There could be no doubt that the caller was important to her daughter.

Lizzie looked across at her at that moment, and Helen looked away quickly. A man was sitting at the next table – unmistakeably a Brit.

"You're so lucky to live here," Helen said loudly, "The weather's just beautiful. And the whole place is so immaculately clean!"

What was she doing, striking up a conversation with a total stranger? But out of the corner of her eye she could see that Lizzie looked relieved.

"I don't live out here, actually," the man said pleasantly. "I'm visiting my son. And daughter-in-law," he added quickly.

"Snap!" Helen said, "Except that I'm visiting my daughter. No son-in-law."

The man smiled and lowered his voice. "Truth to tell, I'm out having tea so as not to be under my daughter-in-law's feet all day. I mean, she's a sweet girl, but my son's at work a lot of the time, and – well, we all know that having guests in the house can be exhausting. So I take myself out quite a lot. I have tea here most afternoons. It's nice and close. They live on the very top floor of that high block over there – the yellow one."

What was she doing, striking up a conversation with a stranger?

"Do they? My daughter lives in the one next door. She's just over there, on the phone," Helen said, trying not to point, "And I know what you mean – I'm here for three weeks, and I think I may be cramping her style…"

The man, who'd introduced himself as Robert, laughed. Shortly afterwards he paid his bill and stood. "Perhaps I'll bump into you again," he said as he left.

Lizzie was very quiet for the rest of the afternoon, and Helen had the greatest difficulty in not asking who had been on the phone.

The next day Lizzie, still looking rather forlorn, had to go into work, and Helen went for a swim and then sat on the balcony writing postcards. She was about to go and make herself a cup of coffee when the phone rang.

"Hello?" she said. ➔

"Oh good, you're in. I tried your mobile but got no answer. It's about the weekend…"

If the voice was anything to go by, the man on the other end of the phone must be very attractive, Helen thought, and it was with some reluctance that she interrupted.

"I'm not Lizzie, I'm afraid, I'm her mother. She's at work." Her next words made a bid for freedom before she could stop them, "And you must be Tom."

"Oh, you sound exactly like Lizzie. She told you about me, then," Tom said, sounding pleased. "I was only ringing her to say that I'm sure there'll be another weekend when we can go to Pete and Sarah's beach house, so she shouldn't worry. I thought she sounded a little bit disappointed. Anyway, I'll try her at work. Thanks."

"I did something dreadful and I'd like to tell someone…"

It clearly wasn't her day for not prying, Helen thought.

"Wait," she said, "Hang on a second. Lizzie was meant to be going away with you this weekend? Did she say she couldn't go? Oh dear, that must have been because of me, but the thing is…" Helen hadn't got a clue what the thing actually was. She looked hastily around and her eye lit on the New Straits Times. *President opens new hotel in Kuantan*, the headline read. "The thing is, Tom, I've just this minute booked to go away myself this weekend. I'd like to see a bit more of the country while I'm here. There's a new hotel in Kuantan. So you see, Lizzie will be all alone this weekend…"

When she'd put the phone down, Helen went back into the kitchen and put the kettle on – she still hadn't had the promised coffee, and she'd probably need it. To fortify herself against the irate – and perfectly justified – phone call she'd soon be getting from Lizzie, concerning meddling mothers.

On an impulse, Helen switched off the kettle, picked up her bag and went out into the hot sunshine, walking the short distance to The Coffee Bean. She sank into a chair and picked up the menu. It was getting a bit late for coffee. Perhaps she'd have lunch here as well.

"May I join you?" Robert said, sitting down a minute later.

"Oh!" Helen felt instantly flustered, and was annoyed with herself. She was pretty sure she was blushing as well. "I thought you usually came here in the afternoons."

"I do. But… well I have to confess that I saw you from our flat. Up there," he said, pointing to a plant-festooned balcony at the top of the yellow building. And I rushed out. I hope you don't mind."

Helen gave a deep sigh. "I don't mind at all. I've just done something dreadful. I'd like to tell someone…"

By the time Helen had finished her confession, their lunch had arrived and Robert was roaring with laughter.

"So next time your phone rings you think you'll be for the high jump, do you?" he asked. Helen nodded. "And have you booked to go to this hotel yet?" he continued. She shook her head dolefully. "Do you even know where Kuantan is? Or how you're going to get there?"

More agonised head shaking.

Robert instantly got out his phone and found the hotel on the internet.

"It looks great. Just look at that beach! I have a confession too: our flat overlooks your pool. I've seen you there – looking very glamorous – so I know you like swimming." He hesitated. "I know this is very forward of me, Helen, but… would you like some company this weekend? We could hire a car. And I'd really like to get to know you better…"

Before he'd finished his sentence, Helen was nodding gratefully, and they'd both started to laugh. At which point Helen's mobile rang.

"Better answer it," Robert said, pulling a mock-frightened face.

"Mum!" Lizzie said so loudly that they could both hear her, "What is this all about? Tom says you're going away for the weekend?"

Helen took a deep breath.

"I am," she said calmly. "I've found that you should grab every chance of happiness that comes your way." She paused, smiled, then added, "We all should." Ⓜ

Spanish Steps

Jenny had loved her working life, but now she was discovering the joy of real living!

By MARIE PENMAN

The heat hit Jenny the second she left the airport, drifting from the cool, almost chilly temperature of the air-conditioned arrivals lounge into a wall of hot air. She was so taken aback, she almost laughed aloud. Obviously, she'd expected Spain to be warmer than the UK in May, but this – this oven? It was like having a hairdryer blowing into her face!

As Jenny wheeled her suitcase across the wide pavement and rummaged in her handbag for her sunglasses, she gazed around, taking in the clean sun-bleached walls of the terminal building and the towering palm trees, but most of all, the sky: so blue and cloud-free, it looked painted. And so big! It seemed to take up much more space than the sky back home, stretching up, down and along the horizon. Spain! Finally, she was here.

At the age of 62, Jenny felt a new chapter beginning in her life, and one that was very different from anything she had expected. Yes, she had always planned to retire in her sixties, having spent her entire career working in the town planning department of her local council, but hadn't really thought about what would come next. Her working days had revolved around meetings, consultations, site visits and reports, with so much packed in that every morning over coffee, Jenny wrote a to-do list in her notebook. Every evening, without fail, she left the office with every item ticked off.

Jenny had never married, though had come close a couple of times, and had no children, which didn't really bother her. It did seem to bother others, especially women – her mum, her sister – who couldn't understand that she had no desire to have a baby of her own. So she

lived alone and genuinely enjoyed her own company. Still, colleagues at her retirement party had teased her, suggesting she'd be bored and begging to come back to work within a month. That hadn't happened.

Instead, she had written another to-do list, made up of things she hoped to achieve during those first few months, and over several weeks, had systematically ticked off the items in her notebook: get a new bathroom fitted, decorate the living room, empty the hall cupboard, tidy up the garden… One final task remained: learn Spanish.

Rachael, a friend from work, had encouraged her. She had studied languages at university and practised basic sentences with Jenny when she had signed up for an evening class at the local college a couple of years earlier. But though she had picked up the basics – learning how to say numbers, colours, days of the week – she had never fully grasped the language.

"You know, Jenny, the best way to learn a foreign language is to live in the country," Rachael had said, as they chatted over lunch one day. "I learned grammar and vocabulary at university, but I only became fluent when I moved to Madrid for my study year abroad." ➞

Jenny had smiled. "That sounds great, Rachael, but it would give me a heck of a long commute to work!"

Rachael had laughed. "I know it doesn't seem possible now, Jen, but who knows what the future might hold?"

Then one day, a few months after she'd retired, Jenny had gone for a check-up at the dentist, and as she'd sat in the waiting room, flicking through magazines, a small advert in the corner of a page had caught her eye: *Learn Spanish in Spain! Intensive language courses for age 50+*

Jenny had glanced around the waiting room to make sure nobody was watching and then without hesitating, had ripped the advert out of the magazine.

When she got home after having her teeth poked and prodded, Jenny opened her laptop and typed in the name of the language school.

The website brought up pictures of sunny beaches, blue skies and small open-air classes, and described intensive language courses lasting either one week, two weeks or four weeks.

Jenny paused for thought. Her house was looking the best it had in years, her garden was neat and tidy and her notebook had no more lists jotted down.

It was time to achieve that final task. She looked back at the website and clicked on the *How to book* link.

Her sister, Liz, and niece, Ella, had been amazed when she'd told them.

"You're going to Spain, Auntie Jen?" Ella had shrieked. "But who with? Where will you live? Who will you talk to?"

Jenny had smiled fondly at this kind young woman, the closest to a daughter she'd ever have. It was hard to believe she was almost thirty herself now.

"I've rented an apartment in Alicante for just over a month," Jenny said. "The classes are in a language school close by – three hours a day, five days a week – and there are activities organised at the weekends too. I'll be fine!"

Liz had hugged her. "I'm so glad you're doing this, Jen. You've worked so hard all your life – it's time to do something just for fun for a change!"

Now, standing alone outside Alicante airport, Jenny couldn't quite believe she was there. She usually went on holidays with Liz and her family, or sometimes just with Ella, though she had taken a few trips alone as well. But this was different. Four weeks in a foreign country, living in a rented apartment and going back to school! First things first, though – getting from the airport into the city centre using public transport...

Using her guide book and her basic Spanish, Jenny found the correct bus for the city, and before long, was standing outside the apartment block she'd found online and booked via email. She liked the look of it immediately – an old stone tenement with a small café bar on the ground floor and wrought iron

> "It's time to do something just for fun for a change!"

balconies all the way up the front of the building. The sea was ten minutes' walk away and the street itself was busy, noisy and bustling. So different from the quiet cul-de-sac she lived in at home.

She collected the apartment key from the caretaker on the first floor and dragged her suitcase up to the third. As she unlocked the front door and pushed it open, she gasped in delight – it was perfect.

Sun flooded in through the double doors that led out on to a tiny balcony, and the apartment was modern and compact – a living/dining room with an open plan kitchen at one end, a big double bedroom and a shining white bathroom. Jenny's first thought was that she wouldn't want to go home at the end of the month!

She dumped her luggage, changed into a cool linen dress and her new leather sandals – yikes, her legs looked so white and bare! – grabbed her handbag and headed out to explore.

First stop, the café bar downstairs, for a glass of delicious freshly-squeezed orange juice and a platter of bread, ham and cheese.

Sitting at a table on the pavement outside, Jenny studied the map in her guidebook and tried to get a sense of the layout of the city. It seemed fairly easy to navigate, especially as the promenade ➤

running along the front of the sea was at the end of every street.

Her classes weren't due to start until Monday, so she had a day and a half to explore the city fully, get some food shopping and break in her new sandals. Jenny smiled at this latest to-do list – so much more enticing than previous pages in her notebook!

Alicante filled her with joy – the beautiful architecture, hidden plazas and quaint churches were so different to what surrounded her back home. And the noise! Everywhere she went, there was loud chatter, music, shouting and laughter. She remembered the teacher at her old evening class saying that if a Spanish child hadn't learned to speak by the age of two, they had no chance, as they'd simply be drowned out by the noise around them.

This was life, as if her senses were open for the first time!

Sitting with a glass of chilled white wine and some tapas in a pavement café on that first evening, Jenny had observed the conversations taking place at the tables around her – lots of people talking over the top of each other, gesticulating and shrieking with laughter. It was normal life, but with the volume turned up much higher!

That first night, she slept soundly and peacefully, waking up early to the noise of crates being delivered to the café downstairs. She pulled on her dressing gown and went out on to the balcony. The sun was rising over the sea, the sky was clear and rosy coloured and it was already warm. It was paradise. Jenny thought back to all the mornings at home when she'd got up in the dark, shivered as she'd driven to work, then returned home in the dark. How did she manage to do that for so long? Liz had asked her about it once, a couple of years ago…

"I know you like your job, Jen, but it's not much of a life, is it? You never see daylight…"

Jenny had smiled. "I'm used to it now. Anyway, what's so great about daylight?" They'd both laughed, and in truth, back then, Jenny had thought being outdoors or getting regular sunshine were over-rated pastimes. Now, though, as she gazed at the sun sparkling over the Mediterranean and smelled the first coffee being brewed downstairs, it was as though her senses were open for the first time. This was life.

She decided to get dressed and go for a walk before breakfast, knowing that it would be stifling later in the day when the temperature rose. She passed the caretaker on the stairs, who gave her a friendly wave, and she practically skipped down the final few steps.

As she walked past the café downstairs, the owner, a friendly man in his forties, recognised her from the day before and called out to her.

"Buenas dias, senora! Como estas?"

Amazingly, Jenny understood what he'd said – so she did learn something at those evening classes after all! – and was even able to respond, "Bien, gracias!"

It was a simple "How are you? I'm fine" exchange, but suddenly, for Jenny, it took on a new and more significant meaning.

As she walked on, adjusting her wide brimmed straw hat and putting on her sunglasses, she realised she was completely fine. Despite initial concerns that her life might be empty and dull without work, she understood now that it could in fact be fuller, maybe even better. What she'd had before was a career. Now, walking by the sea, feeling the heat of the sun on her limbs and looking forward to starting her new class tomorrow, she had a life.

Or rather, una vida.

Jenny smiled to herself.

She mentally made a short to-do list for today: find a nice place for lunch, check out the location of the language school so she'd be able to find her way tomorrow, and finally, send a postcard to Rachael, her former colleague.

She already knew what she'd write on it and could imagine Rachael's surprise when she found it on her desk in their old shared office: *You were right – living in a foreign country is the best way to learn a language!*

Jenny kept walking and a thought sprang into her mind: viva la vida! Long live life. Ⓜ

Getting Away From It All

As exhausted new parents, Claire and Jack sometimes imagine different lives…

By DELLA GALTON

Claire finned through the crystal waters of the Atlantic, her eyes wide behind the clear goggles. Dozens of bright blue fish had just swerved around in her in a graceful shoal.

She was a mermaid. She was on her way to a tryst with a handsome merman at a romantic underwater ball, where the stage was made from mother of pearl and the band played conches and clam shell guitars.

The merman was a prince. They would dance all night while crab waiters served food on tiny white plates, and all the beautiful people of the sea gathered to celebrate their love.

She was a mermaid and… Ouch!

She'd snagged her fingers against a rough piece of rock on the seabed. The beautiful images wavered and shivered in her mind's eye like a reflection in water on a summer's day when someone has just lobbed a stone.

She was not a beautiful mermaid with a flat stomach and a jewelled tail. She was a mum of two under-fives, with a slightly podgy tummy and wobbly thighs. And she was snorkelling on holiday.

She came up for air. It was beautiful here, though. It was the first time they had come on a family holiday. It was the first time they'd been able to afford to – she and Jack, her merman.

Jack was currently in sole charge of Olivia and Liam. She should probably get back and check that he was OK.

Jack was feeling the heat. And the stress. They had been building a sandcastle but then Olivia had knocked a turret off with her pudgy baby fingers and Liam had kicked sand over her.

She had some in her eye and was inconsolable.

Liam was unapologetic.

"Wasn't my fault," he yelled when Jack told him to apologise. "She was in the way."

Happy holidays, Jack thought, cuddling his daughter and scanning the frill of the tide. Claire had been gone a little while. She was probably making the most of her freedom. Good for her.

"Want Mummy!" Olivia yelled, her voice rising in a wail so that the people on the next sun loungers glanced round disapprovingly.

Just for a second, Jack wished he were back at work in the air-conditioned peace of his office…

But then he thought, oh my goodness, would he really have preferred to be at work than in Tenerife with his family? What kind of dad did that make him?

➜

Claire abandoned the snorkelling, rolled onto her back and floated for a while looking up at the eternal blue. Five more minutes and then she'd go and check on them all.

Her parents had offered to have the children this week. "So you two can have a proper break," her mum had said. "You deserve one."

"It's fine, Mum, we'll take them," Claire had said. "It'll be lovely. But thank you."

From her vantage point she could see most of the beach. But the figures were blurred without her glasses. She couldn't make out her own little family. A cloud passed over the sun and, suddenly missing them, she decided to head back.

Jack looked mightily relieved to see her when she returned. He passed her a still-crying Olivia and muttered something about needing to go to the toilet.

"Take Liam with you to get an ice cream," she called after him. But he was already gone, striding across the beach, as if he couldn't get away fast enough.

"We'll get ice cream in a minute," Claire told a frustrated Liam, who'd puckered his lips to yell. Olivia had stopped crying at the sound of her favourite word.

Claire found some bottled water to bathe her eye, just to make sure the sand was out. Her daughter smelled of sun cream and seaside.

She hugged her tight.

Jack struggled through the crowds on the wide plaza. He was no longer a father of two, gritty-eyed with tiredness – he hadn't slept last night because Olivia was fractious and he'd known that Claire was exhausted.

He was a warrior. He was hacking his way through a thicket, a jungle of people, with predators coming at him from every turn. The woman with the buggy, who was too distracted to notice where she was going; the old lady on the scooter; the child with the plastic sword – *olé!* he crowed inside his head.

He was a primeval hunter-gatherer, off to find food for his family, just as soon as he'd killed the monsters. Oh – and paid a visit to the gents. He was a man on a mission.

On the beach, Claire had kissed Olivia's eye better and was supervising Liam, who was now building an underground tunnel to the sea.

The tide was coming in fast. Soon the beach would be a thin, dark strip of sand. Claire was aware of her children's fragile skin. They both wore T-shirts and sun hats. Was that enough?

It was a major adventure to come down to the main beach. Maybe tomorrow they should stay a bit closer to the apartment.

She saw Jack heading back. He was holding cones, two to a hand. Liam spotted him too.

"Ice-creams!" he yelled.

At just after four they headed back to their apartment.

Her mother had offered to take the children to give them a break

"It's long enough, isn't it?" Claire said, touching Jack's arm. "You look worn out, love. Why don't you go and have a snooze while I sort out their tea?"

He smiled at her. "We could get you an ice-cream from the kiosk if you like?"

Olivia's cornet had ended up face-down in the sand when she'd only had two licks so Claire had donated hers.

"It'll be better for my waistline," she had quipped. Now she said, "Maybe I will."

But she didn't.

In their apartment she bathed the children, and then she made toast from the sweet Spanish bread and heated up a can of spaghetti hoops in tomato sauce she'd found in the Super Mercado.

This was what happened at home, Claire thought ruefully. One or other of them would look after the children while the other caught up on sleep. That's what it was like, her mum had said once, when you →

had two children under five.

"It won't always be like this, love."

But it was a far cry from the dream Claire had had of motherhood.

When the kids were finally fed and settled, Claire pushed open the door of their bedroom a fraction. She could hear Jack snoring gently. Bless him. He'd gone out like a light.

She pulled the door closed a crack. In a bit she would have a shower, then maybe she would sit on the balcony of their apartment and catch her breath. Have a moment where she was no longer a mother, or a mermaid, or a wife, but just Claire, on holiday, taking a moment to herself.

It was a far cry from the dream Claire had had of motherhood

She had just poured herself a glass of wine, when Jack appeared, yawning and tousled.

"Hiya, love. Sorry, I didn't mean to sleep for so long. I wanted to help with the bedtime stories."

"There's always tomorrow." She smiled tenderly at him and gestured to the second glass of wine beside hers. "As long as one of us is awake."

He sat beside her. "We're both on catch up. We'll feel human again by tomorrow."

"Or maybe the next day," she teased.

"Maybe."

"Jack, do you ever imagine that you're someone else… a fictional character, living another life?"

He raised his eyebrows and she giggled as she explained.

"Today while I was snorkelling, I imagined I was a mermaid going to a mermaid's ball under the sea."

"I imagined I was a warrior," Jack said. "Back in the days when that meant killing dinosaurs and hunting for food."

"Does that mean we actually want different lives?" she murmured, a trace wistfully.

"No, it means we've been watching too much kiddies' television.

I like my life, actually."

"I like my life too."

Jack leaned forward and brushed a stray tendril of hair from her face. "Tomorrow we will go to a ball, and you will be my princess and I will be your prince."

She laughed. "A ball?"

"OK, a dinner," he conceded. "The table is booked." He hesitated. "You know, I'm glad we didn't leave the kids with your mum and dad."

"Me, too," she said. "Although I'm also glad Mum and Dad came with us. It's the best of both worlds, isn't it?" She rested her head against his shoulder. "It's lovely of them to offer to babysit."

She'd meant it, she realised, about loving her life.

Love was a funny thing   it was about Jack looking after Olivia when she had a nightmare so Claire could sleep. It was about her, handing over her ice-cream with a smile.

It was about knowing that one day they'd look back on this as their first family holiday. Where they built sandcastles and dreams.

They clinked glasses, perfectly in tune with each other.

"Here's to us," Jack said softly.

"To us," Claire repeated with a smile. 🅜

Say Cheese!

The pungent smell brought back memories of a place that meant so much to her

By JO THOMAS

It was the smell she recognised straight away. A smell that took her right back to a time and a place. Lottie looked at the parcel and smiled. Cheese! Lottie loved cheese. It was one of the things she loved most about living here in the Alpine mountains. The cows and the cheese.

"What's that pong?" she heard her flatmate call from her bedroom. Lottie smiled. It must have been her. Trying to cheer her up. The people closest to her knew how much she loved cheese. For some it's chocolate when they need a lift, for Lottie, it was cheese. Lottie smiled. Who else would know that she needed cheering up today?

"I'm off to work," her flatmate Alice called. "See you later. Looks lovely out there today!"

Lottie looked out of the window from their shared apartment in the hotel, over the mountains, the deep green grass and the forest of tall pines. She looked back at the parcel that had arrived at reception this morning. She opened the brown package slowly, inhaling the smell that strengthened as she pulled back the brown paper.

She held it to her nose again and inhaled, keeping her eyes closed as she did, letting time stand still just for a moment, enjoying a memory. She drew it back from her face, opened her eyes and looked again at the parcel.

There was no note at all. She took another look at the cheese. It was exactly the same. She took another sniff, the smell of the cheese, curled up and around her little apartment, wrapping around her, like a hug.

She knew exactly what she was going to do today! She didn't want

to mope around. She needed to get outside, in the sunshine, among the trees. She knew exactly where she was going to go and what she was going to do after her shift today.

When the clock finally clicked round to five o'clock, she quickly packed a few things into her rucksack and headed outside. She looked around from the wooden balcony of the hotel, over the mountains, breathing in the beautiful fresh air.

This place was heaven in winter and summer. Winter for the skiers who flocked to the slopes and in the summer sunshine, there was watersports and walkers enjoying the Swiss air, hills, trees and mountain cows grazing on the lush green slopes.

It had been a now or never moment when she'd decided to stay on. And she was so glad she had, that this was her now. Leaving behind life in a busy city bar to take a job as a chalet host, and then to stay on as assistant manager in the hotel had seemed madness to a lot of her friends. But to her, it felt exactly right.

There was only one thing that could make this beautiful setting ➞

any better. But it had been three months since the end of the skiing season and Nick's job as a chef in a large lodge had come to an end. Three months to the day, he'd returned to the UK to work in his dad's pub and they'd agreed to part, not to make it hard on each other, because they had no idea how or when they could be together again.

Lottie walked down the steps of the hotel, greeting holidaymakers as she went, holding her face to the still warm glorious sunshine. She headed away from the hotel and up towards the forest, the smell of the trees drawing her in, with only the sound of fallen twigs under her feet, the sound of cows mooing in the background, her feet seemingly following a path of their own, knowing exactly where they were going.

Back to a secret, favourite spot off the main walking routes. She first found it when she'd been offered the job at the hotel and was deciding whether to stay on, turning to the trees to help her clear her thoughts, breath in the clean air and giving her time to think. And it was where she'd come back to when she needed time to stand still and to capture the moment, just as she had three months ago when Nick and her had said their final goodbyes.

As she walked she could feel her spirits lift. They always did here in woods and on the hillsides.

Eventually she arrived at the clearing. It was as perfect as she always remembered. Cool in the shade of the trees around three sides, and then nothing but rolling hillsides, and a view down to the town below and the mountains beyond that.

She sat on a wooden log, beside the stone circle of a firepit and unpacked her rucksack. The cheese in its paper, she placed on a big flat stone there that served as a perfect kitchen table. Then she collected some dry sticks and leaves and gathered them into the fire pit, putting a bottle of water beside it. Then she pulled out her box of matches and struck one, held the flame to the dry wood, and watched it as it caught and flared. Now all she had to do was sit back and wait.

She looked out over the beautiful view, remembering every moment of the last time she and Nick were together. Knowing their winter season had come to and end and savouring every moment of it.

She stared at the flames taking hold on the little fire she'd built and fed it with fallen sticks. Then she looked out at the view again in front of her, looking over the mountains, when she heard footsteps behind her. At first she jumped and then smiled. It must be Alice coming to join her after her shift she thought.

"Hope you brought wine." Lottie smiled not turning round, but tending the little fire.

"I did, as it happens. And bread," said the familiar voice.

Her heart leapt, and her stomach flipped over and back again. Slowly she turned, a ripple of excitement running around her body, and stared. "It's you!" she caught her breath! "You sent the cheese! You remembered!"

"Of course!"

With that he came and sat beside her on another log.

Both of them staring at each other, smiling, as if unsure what to do next.

She lifted the skillet pan she'd carried up there in her rucksack and held up the cheese. And from his rucksack, he produced a picnic hamper with a bottle of wine and loaf of rustic, crusty bread, neither saying a word, letting the actions do the talking.

She could feel her spirits lift, as they always did in among the trees

She pulled out a clove of garlic from her bag, a small penknife, halved it and rubbed the inside of the skillet pan, then chopped the clove and added it to the pan, as he handed her the bottle of wine.

She took it, her hands shaking slightly, and as his fingertips touched hers she felt a shock of excitement run through her body. She splashed some of the wine into the pan, just as they'd done before, the day they'd said goodbye. And then, handing it back to him, he produced two plastic glasses and filled them, handing her one, just as before.

She took the cheese, tearing it into pieces in her lap and dipping it into a bag of cornflour, and as the wine simmered over the open fire, she dropped the cheese into the pan, until it thickened, making sure ➞

it didn't boil. Then she put the pan between them, on the big flat stone and took a sip of wine. He handed her a chunk of crusty bread with that familiar smile that kept lighting her up when he did.

"After you," he said.

She tore a piece of the loaf he'd given her and dipped it into the warm, gooey, stringy fondue and bit into it. She was right back there, in the setting sun, just like the day they'd said goodbye.

"I didn't know if you'd remember…..about this place. The fondue," he finally said, after many mouthfuls of the pungent garlicky scoops of cheese on the bread, and having taken a sip of the wine.

"I did." Tears sprang to her eyes. How could she not remember? This was where they had said goodbye. A scene imprinted on her memory. Then, scooping another mouthful of cheese and bread, while trying to get her thoughts straight and swallowing, almost not daring to ask, her emotions all over the place. Why was he here? Was he alone? She said tentatively, "Are you back as a guest?"

This was where they had said goodbye, to lead separate lives

"No," he replied just as tentatively.

"No?" she raised her eyebrow. She hadn't expected to be sitting here this evening, eating fondue, looking out over the setting sun, with Nick.

"Clearly you haven't heard! Too busy working and no phone signal up here," he smiled gently. "Tom, the main chef for the big lodge," he said, still dipping bread into cheese. "He's only gone and broken his arm mountain biking. The family thought of me, after working out here this winter with him."

It was like deja vue, the day they had sat here when she had been offered the job at the hotel and his contract had run its course; when they had known their time together had come to an end. He was going back to the UK to work in his dad's pub for the summer in Swn Y Mor. She had a chance to stay on and get promoted. They had sat, eaten fondue, and drunk wine before finally saying goodbye, knowing it was right for both of them.

"Would you mind?" he asked again tentatively.

This time the tears that sprung to her eyes spilled over. She couldn't speak. She brushed away the tears and shook her head, a lot. He smiled. She sniffed and laughed.

It was like no time had passed at all.

"And your dad's pub?"

"It's lovely, but it doesn't have what this place has," he said.

"What, trees, mountain air, ski runs in the winter?" She looked out and then back at him.

"You," he replied, leaning towards her. "I can't think of anyone else I want to eat fondue with."

"And will there be more fondue if you take the job?" she smiled through her watery, joyful tears.

"As much as you like…" He leaned in closer to her. She could feel his breath on her lips.

"In that case," she said leaning towards him, "I'd like that very much."

And together then leant further towards each other until finally their lips met, again, just like they had said goodbye, their lips saying all they needed to say, and now here they were, saying hello, just as clearly.

As they drew apart, he smiled at her.

The sun was setting over the mountains pushing out it's rays towards them. Neither of them knew exactly what was round the corner, but they were on the journey together.

And for better or for worse, there was always cheese. Ⓜ

A Souvenir From Greece

Stacey brought more than a fridge magnet this time, hoping Mum would understand...

By MHAIRI GRANT

My mum looked at the fridge magnet as if it was a nugget of gold. Then she re-arranged her existing magnets on the fridge door to make room for it. There were windmills from the Netherlands, Flamenco Dancers from Barcelona, the Parthenon in Athens, the Eiffel Tower and the Berlin Bear, as well as numerous dog magnets.

Now she had a turtle one from the Greek island of Zakynthos where turtles lay their eggs on Laganas and Kalamaki beaches.

"So, I take it you had a good holiday? You certainly have a lovely tan."

I went with my friend and we had a... disagreement but I was not about to tell Mum that. Nor the fact that careful me had maxed out my credit card. Especially as I had my cousin's wedding coming up.

"I'll put the kettle on and you can tell me all about it."

Keep calm, Stacey I told myself, keep calm. But a little voice said that I should have consulted Mum first. After all, I had moved back in with her six months ago when I had broken up with Steve. But, once again I had let my heart rule my head.

Over a cuppa I gave her an edited version of my holiday; the food, the sights, the clubs, the beaches and a sighting of a turtle in the sea.

"But no holiday romance?"

That's the trouble with mums – they know when you're holding out on them.

"No," I said firmly, but I was thinking about hair flopping over a pair of liquid brown eyes, and so I changed the subject.

"How's the wedding coming along? Has Susie got her wedding dress?"

"Yes, and it is absolutely gorgeous, talking of which we'll have to shop for our outfits soon."

"What's it like?" I asked, evading the issue of shopping, knowing that I couldn't afford anything now.

I relaxed as my mum described the wedding dress. I'll tell her tomorrow, I thought, after a good night's sleep. But my mum stopped and looked at me.

"What is it, you are not telling me, Stacey?"

Are you mad? I can almost hear Rhona's words. My friend shook her head and told me to think twice. Instead of answering I reached for my phone and clicked on the pictures. She smiled as she swiped through them and then she stopped.

"Who's that?" Mum asked.

"That's Stavros, he wanted to take Rhona out on his boat. But Rhona told him that she was no Shirley Valentine."

"She's got her head screwed on that girl."

Silly, I know, but I felt an implied criticism. I had once been described as a soft touch, and my relationship with Steve seemed to confirm it. I had a good job but Steve had made a big hole in my savings with his nefarious schemes. He would have left me destitute if I had not finally given him the heave. Mum said little about the split other than, *thank God you didn't marry him.*

→

My mum began to smile and I knew the reason why. Two days into my holiday I met a local and he was in nearly every photo.

"Oh, he's so cute!"

Her reaction gave me hope. Still, I felt my hands go cold with nerves. Mum had welcomed me with love back into her home, and now I was about to take advantage of that love. "I call him, Rusty."

"Call?"

Not the past tense – she was quick, my mum. I cleared my throat. "Yes, beneath the dirt he was a burnt orange colour. When I first saw him, he was so hungry…"

"Just ignore him," Rhona had said, "If you feed him then you won't get rid of him."

But I couldn't ignore the dog. He followed me everywhere. He was a young dog with a hard life written all over him. He had fleas, sticking-out ribs and a suppurating sore on one of his legs. I took him to a local vet.

"He has a lovely nature, Mum and he scrubbed up well. I… I couldn't just leave him. I'm sorry I should have consulted you first but–"

"You're bringing him here?"

"Yes, an ex-pat couple are looking after him just now but I've made arrangements for him to be flown over. He has a lovely nature, Mum and he's so biddable. I… I couldn't just leave him."

Mum continued to look at his picture, the one with his tongue hanging out and his bright eyes, his happy face. The face of a dog who was being looked after and loved for the first time in short, sad life. I couldn't take that away from him. I couldn't.

"What do you think, Mum?"

She'd had dogs for most of her life – until two years ago when her beloved Sheba died. I know she would understand my sentiment, but it was a huge commitment.

"It sure beats a fridge magnet," she with tears in her eyes, "Rusty… I can hardly wait to meet him."

"I love you, Mum," I said hugging her.

Rusty, Mum and me – he was going to be one spoiled dog. Ⓜ

A Holiday For Everyone

Blending two families as one was going to be more complex than they'd thought

By SUE MOORCROFT

Nice room, eh, Shannon?"

Dawn beamed. She was determined not to make an issue of sharing with her daughter, even though the holiday had been intended as a "next step" in Dawn's relationship with Jason.

They'd met at a party a few months ago and the sparks between them had almost lit up the room. Jason wanted a shared future and it was delicious to feel wanted again after ten years divorced – but she'd never hurt fourteen-year-old Shannon.

Shannon grinned back as she dropped her backpack on a bed.

"Looks awesome." ➝

Dawn opened the sliding door and stepped out onto the balcony, taking a deep breath of sun-drenched air.

"Gorgeous view! The older buildings in Malta look golden in the sunlight."

Shannon bounced out to join her.

"It's loads warmer than at home. The hotel's beach club is across the road, isn't it? Can we go?"

"Soon, I should think." Dawn was conscious that for once there wasn't only herself and her daughter to consider.

Shannon did seem to like Jason and his three cheery, brown-haired daughters, Kelly, Christina and Kimberley. Kelly was just younger than Shannon and Christina and Kimberley older.

But they'd hit a bump in the road when Jason had said, "Shannon fits right in. We'd love it if you'd come to Malta with us. We go every year. Christina can share with Kimberley and Shannon with Kelly."

It wasn't the sun bouncing off the blue Mediterranean that made Dawn close her eyes now. It was the memory of Shannon's white face as she'd answered stiffly, "I'd like my own room."

Jason had scratched his head. "We can really only afford three twin rooms, sweetheart. It would cost loads for you to have a room alone."

Shannon had blinked and replied, "Then you share with Kelly. I'll share with Mum."

Parental sleeping arrangements were best not discussed in detail with teenagers and they hadn't been able to cajole her into any other arrangement, except she'd offered to stay with her dad while the rest of them went to Malta, which Dawn had resisted. The last thing she wanted for Shannon was isolation.

Jason appeared on the next balcony, rubbing in sun cream.

"My lot want to go down to the beach club," he announced.

"So do we," Dawn said, happy that everyone seemed in accord.

"Race you there," Shannon cried, spinning on her heel.

Before long, the four girls were splashing and shrieking in the pool while Jason and Dawn reclined on blue loungers drinking cocktails and gazing out to sea. Jason took Dawn's hand.

"They're mixing a bit. I don't suppose Shannon will relent on the sleeping arrangements?"

She smiled at him over her sunglasses. "I know you'd have preferred we were together but it's early days. Let's not make a fuss."

He grinned. "OK. I'm used to my three being adaptable, I suppose. Shannon's a typical only child."

Dawn pointed out lightly, "Yours are typical children-with-siblings."

The beach club was perfect. They could get snacks and drinks from the bar, swim, or just relax and watch white boats bobbing out to sea.

The four teenagers looked young and vibrant with their wet pony tails and bright bikinis, but Dawn felt uneasy at the way Shannon seemed to keep herself apart, pale and shy while the others were loud and boisterous.

Shannon didn't want to share a room with any of his daughters

As if reading her thoughts, Jason murmured, "I know we haven't talked to the girls yet about moving in together but with the fees associated with selling our houses, I don't see how we could run to one with five bedrooms so each girl could have one to herself."

"No," she replied, giving Shannon a thumbs-up across the pool as she broke the surface after a neat dive.

"And it doesn't seem fair to get mine to share when she won't."

"True."

She smiled but her cocktail suddenly tasted sour.

Jason was a good man, a factory manager with the responsibility to make things work. Shannon sharing with his daughter on holiday had made sense to him – and he was hinting strongly that the same would be true at home.

However, Dawn could understand that Shannon had her own room now, so why should she change?

Kimberley, Kelly and Christina shared. In their modest semi, Jason had knocked a double and a single into one, cleverly making use of the space to give them a bed and desk each. Shannon had gaped ➤

when she'd seen everyone's possessions jumbled together and the girls sitting on each other's beds.

Dawn realised she might have to put the brakes on Jason's enthusiasm for making two families into one. Some of the warmth seemed to go out of the sunshine.

Later, they gathered their things to go back to their rooms and change. "We usually go to the restaurant on the corner on the first night," Jason said.

"OK," Dawn replied.

Shannon waited a beat. "If you like."

The meal was delicious. Dawn relaxed as the wine went down and the girls laughed and joked together. Shannon listened more than she spoke, but that was just her way.

After the meal, Kimberley, whose nose was already looking sun-kissed, asked, "OK if we look in the shops that stay open late by Sliema Creek?"

She didn't have to say she'd put Shannon first – it's what parents did

"Of course," Jason replied. But when they reached the corner where the traffic rumbled past and the black, slack water of the creek reflected golden light, he patted Shannon's shoulder, slowing his steps so she automatically let the others draw ahead. "I'm glad we're getting to know each other."

"Why?" Shannon tilted her chin in a gesture Dawn recognised. Her daughter was wary.

Jason looked wrong-footed.

"Because I like you very much and I hope you're going to fit in with my three girls."

Shannon fixed her eyes dreamily on the nearest boat tied to the quay. "In Citizenship at school we've been talking about democracy versus equality. In democracy, if five people vote yes and one votes no then the five get their way." She switched her gaze to Jason.

"But equality's not about one person having to change in order to 'fit in' with everyone else because that suits the majority. It's about everyone's views being equally important." With a polite smile she followed the others towards the late-night shops.

The silence she left behind was loud.

"I made a mess of that." Jason sounded winded.

Dawn took his hand. "She's right, though," she murmured sadly. "I want to be with you but she's happy as we are. It's nice of your girls to be welcoming, but what if that's not what she wants? Why should she accommodate our happiness at the expense of hers?"

The eyes he turned on her were wounded. "Good to know your views. Sorry if I've jumped on anyone's corns."

They followed Shannon to the shops full of beach dresses and straw hats and the rest of the evening passed with them being polite to one another. Dawn was glad she wasn't sharing a room with Jason after all.

In the morning, Jason was sheepish. "I've hardly slept," he murmured to Dawn in the breakfast buffet queue. "I didn't mean to be insensitive to Shannon's feelings. I'd just love us all to be one family."

"I know, but we've gone about things the wrong way," she whispered, shuffling aside to let a sunburned woman reach a yogurt. "We even brought her to a holiday destination you guys already know and love, but it's just foreign to her. If blending our families is going to work, we need to show her she counts."

He looked at her in horror. "If?"

She nodded. She didn't have to say she'd put Shannon first. He'd put his kids first if a situation arose that warranted it. That's what parents did.

"I'm not trying to crowd you into acting a certain way, but at team-building meetings at work we're always being told to listen to every member of the team, even the quiet ones."

"Good point," he said reflectively. "But if Shannon enjoys this holiday, maybe she'll begin to enjoy being part of a larger family."

"Maybe," Dawn agreed, as they carried their trays to the table ➥

the girls had already claimed.

They sat down and when there was a break in the conversation, Jason said, "Dawn and I would like everyone to take turns choosing things this holiday. Want to go first, Shannon? What would you like to do after breakfast?"

Her eyebrows rose.

"Back to the pool this morning, then McDonald's for lunch?" she suggested.

Dawn pinched her lips together. Jason was not a burger fan! But if blending their families was to have any hope...

Smiling, he took Dawn's hand beneath the table.

"Great, we'll do that. Then maybe Kelly can choose what we do in the afternoon and Kimberley and Christina tomorrow?"

Everybody agreed – except Shannon.

"But that order's illogical. Maybe we should go in age so that would make Kelly first, me next, then Christina, then Kimberley and then you and Mum."

"That's fair," Dawn put in swiftly, keen that Jason should notice Shannon was not asking for special treatment. She just didn't want to be overlooked.

But he was already nodding, brown eyes twinkling. "You're a real diplomat, Shannon."

Shannon flashed him a smile and her shoulders seemed to relax.

The conversation moved on but Dawn's heart soared. This moment had been a turning point.

Blending families was a slower, more complex exercise then she'd thought. Everyone had to adjust – including Jason – but that didn't mean it wasn't going to work.

"I think we're going to have a wonderful holiday!" she sighed.

And everyone agreed. Even Shannon. 🄼🅆

Just Cruising

A spur of the moment decision on a rainy day changed Veronica's life forever

By JAN SNOOK

The dragonfly settled on the lily pad, its iridescent wings sparkling in the August sunshine. Veronica watched it as she sipped her coffee, enjoying the sun on her bare legs.

What a difference six months made! She smiled wryly at the thought. In the first months of the year there had hardly been a dry day for weeks on end. Every night the news was full of record rainfalls and the resultant flooding.

The dragonfly took off suddenly, and began to patrol the garden. Such a sense of purpose, so single-minded. She smiled again, thinking of her daughter, Anna.

Brisk, efficient Anna had always known her own mind. She'd worked for the same company since she left school, rising quickly up the ranks, dedicating every waking hour to her job. ➔

The office was conveniently close to her parents' house so she had never bothered – or really had time – to leave home. Then, when Roger had died, it had been a comfort to Veronica to have her there.

She supposed she should have tried a bit harder to encourage Anna to fly the nest, but... well, anyway, she hadn't. Then suddenly Anna was thirty-seven and Veronica realised guiltily that the time for her to leave home might have passed.

Until, that was, last summer.

Anna's boss, the managing director, was about to retire and she had applied for his job. For weeks before the selection process Anna stayed at the office late every night, then after several promising interviews they waited on tenterhooks for Head Office to reach a decision.

On the appointed day Veronica jumped each time the phone rang, expecting it to be Anna, and leapt to her feet when she at last heard Anna's key in the lock.

Even before Veronica had made it to the fridge to fetch the waiting bottle of fizz, Anna's wail reached her.

It was clear that they were utterly besotted with each other

"They've offered it to some unknown man! They said it was a hard decision but that I was too young! They said..." But what they said was lost in Veronica's commiserating hug, and the tears that Anna had held at bay all day.

For the next few days Anna did what could only be described as sulk. For hard-working Anna, this took the form of leaving the office at six instead of nine or ten, and sometimes taking a walk in the park in her lunch hour instead of forgetting to eat lunch altogether.

She talked of finding another job, of leaving the area, of turning her life around. And after a while Veronica realised Anna was making some of the changes she'd talked of. Her hair looked different, and there was a bit of a spring in her step.

Actually, when Veronica looked at her more closely, there was a definite bloom to her cheeks, and she seemed to be splashing out a bit on new clothes. Well, good! She hadn't taken the disappointment too much to heart, then.

The name of the new managing director began to come up in conversation a little more often: Mr Thompson thinks this, Alex Thompson thinks that, Alex wants to make changes, Alex and I are thinking of doing such and such. The "Alex and I" sentences began to sound a bit on the breathy side, and were always accompanied by a smile, sometimes even a blush... And Anna was staying late at the office again.

It took until late October for Anna to suggest she might bring Alex home to meet Veronica. On the appointed evening Anna looked her mother up and down, adjusted her collar and gave a jerky little nod of approval, before answering the door and letting Alex in.

It was clear that they were utterly besotted with each other, and Veronica was not in the least surprised when they announced their engagement that very evening.

O nce the ball was rolling, there was no stopping them. Anna and Alex were married in the village church soon after Christmas, and went off on honeymoon without a care in the world.

Strange, really, Veronica mused, that the office that had taken up Anna and Alex's every waking moment not long ago, could suddenly function perfectly well without either of them for two whole weeks...

And how fortunate they were to be away that particular fortnight. The heavens opened almost the moment they got on the plane and didn't let up. The house felt oddly empty, and for the first time the future seemed a little bleak.

For goodness' sake, pull yourself together, Veronica told herself sternly the second time she caught herself dwelling on her impending isolation. It's just the weather getting you down. Everyone's miserable. They'll only be a couple of miles away. And you'll be able to do exactly as you like: you can have cornflakes for supper if you want to, in front of the television!   ➔

The day before Anna and Alex were due back, Veronica bought a few essentials – milk, bread and so forth – for their return, intending to deliver them to Alex's rented riverside cottage in the neighbouring village, where they were to start married life.

She was just leaving when the phone rang. It was Alex's neighbour to say that the cottage – and in fact most of the village – was flooded. Their whole ground floor was awash!

Veronica spent the day doing what she could, then came home and made endless phone calls. Even when the water receded, it would be weeks before the house was habitable again.

It was no way to start married life, Veronica reflected sadly as she finally came off the phone. Anna had lived with her for long enough. Surely she should be allowed to settle into life with Alex without this sort of complication.

In the short term, of course, both of them moving in with her was the most practical solution, while their own house was drying out. There were no other houses to rent as close to their office as hers was, and she had plenty of room.

Even so… Veronica sat down in front of the television still wondering what she would do, and half-heartedly listening to the weather forecast. Yet more rain! She was fed up with it. The next programme began: yet another reality TV show. She switched it off and went to make a cup of tea instead. What she could do with was a bit of sunshine.

It took her a moment to realise that was the solution. She should go away. She could go on a nice long cruise, leaving Anna and Alex in her house while they sorted out what they were going to do.

She almost skipped back into the sitting-room and began flicking furiously through the paper. She'd seen an ad…

It had worked out perfectly. Alex and Anna had been back a week from their honeymoon, and Veronica was half way across the Atlantic.

She had booked at the very last minute, so it had been a bit of a bargain really. Well, a lot less than she'd been expecting. In two days' time the ship would dock in New York – and from there they would head for the Caribbean. She'd already caught herself humming calypso music in the shower in her rather swish cabin bathroom. She could hardly wait!

The only slight – and really, it was very slight – disappointment was her table in the restaurant. The food was unbelievable – and so much choice! – but she had found herself on a table of... singletons, she supposed they were called these days. There were eight of them on the table, according to the seating plan, but so far she'd only met six of the others, and she was at least twenty years older than any of them. Not that they weren't pleasant, it was just that she often didn't understand what they were talking about.

Veronica glanced at her watch. It was almost half past seven; she ought to go down to dinner.

She dressed carefully – that was

A cruise was the perfect solution to their housing problem

another thing she was enjoying as it made a change to get dressed up – and made her way to the dining-room. There were always lots of things to do after dinner – shows and so forth – and there were lots of people of her own age to talk to then.

She crossed the room, smiling determinedly at the least comprehensible man on her table. When she reached him, however, she found he'd started talking to an attractive man a few years older than she was.

"Hello, I'm David Masters," the newcomer said, turning to her. "I'm afraid it always takes me a day or two to get my sea legs. I believe we're on the same table. I've just been talking to this gentleman –" But the young man in question had turned to speak to someone else. "I'm afraid I can't remember his name," David said in a conspiratorial whisper. "I scarcely understood a syllable he uttered."

Veronica hooted with laughter. "I've been having that problem all week! I thought I was just me."

➤

"Nonsense," David said. "It's these young people. They mumble."

The cruise, Veronica reflected, had taken a very definite turn for the better. That night she and David went to watch a show together, and in New York they went ashore together, only just making it back before the ship sailed.

By the time they reached Barbados the other passengers treated them as an item, and when they reached Jamaica they had started making plans to see each other back home.

The days passed gloriously slowly. When they were ashore, she and David took leisurely meals together, shopped in picturesque markets and swam in tropical coves. On board they enjoyed the same shows, and talked for hours over cocktails. They even danced! Veronica couldn't remember when she'd last danced.

The cruise had taken a very definite turn for the better

The last wonderful evening was tinged with dismay as they both realised that the next day, they'd be back in England.

You must be glad to be back," Alex said over his shoulder as he took Veronica's suitcase into the hall.

And she was. So glad to be back on terra firma – not just in the sense of being on dry land, but also known territory. Even if it did mean that she had to start worrying that her shipboard romance would turn out to be just that; a passing fancy, ships that passed in the night.

Not that it would if she had anything to do with it. She knew where her heart lay. Maybe she could give him a ring, find out if he'd got home safely. Women did that these days, didn't they? They didn't wait for the man to ring. Did they?

Goodness, it was a long, long time since she'd been in this position; she didn't know the rules any more!

"You must be tired after your journey," Anna said. "I'll go and put the kettle on. Or maybe you could," she said apologetically as the phone began to ring, "That's probably for me. I'm afraid it may take a few days for our friends to realise we're back in our own house."

Veronica raised her eyebrows, but went obediently into the kitchen. The presumption of youth. Well, relative youth, anyway.

Anna followed her almost immediately, holding out the phone.

"It's for you," she said, her voice pregnant with curiosity.

Veronica's heart leapt. She had, of course, hoped it might be.

"I was just ringing to check you'd got home safely."

His voice sounded like chocolate. Maybe it always did, and she just hadn't noticed until she hadn't heard it for a day.

Her heart did a little jig. Not just a holiday romance, then!

Anna was looking at her strangely, and she realised she was grinning.

Now he was inviting himself down the day after tomorrow, talking about staying in a local pub.

"Oh no," Veronica told him, "You must stay with me. There's plenty of room."

She hung up feeling euphoric.

"David will be here on Tuesday," she said as nonchalantly as she could, considering Anna was practically shining a searchlight in her eyes. "I met him on the cruise. We... got on rather well. You'll be back in your own house by then, won't you?"

"Well, I hope so, Mum. Do you think I should book a room for this David at the Coach and Horses – just in case? It will be crowded if we're all here."

The excited jig stopped abruptly and Veronica's heart began to sink. She could feel herself about to agree when her son-in-law interrupted.

"No, of course not. Your mother's given up her house for quite long enough. I'm sure our house will be habitable, and if it isn't, then we'll book in at the pub," he said, looking seriously at Veronica. "I would hate to cramp your style," he added gently, "And am I right in thinking that we may be seeing a lot more of this David?"

Veronica looked at them both. "I do hope so. But not perhaps on this occasion. Too early to meet the parents."

"Meet the parents?" Anna asked with a bit of a shriek.

➜

"You know what I mean."

In the event they did meet him. Veronica had the impression that Anna was loitering with intent. Alex was trying to coax her into the car when David arrived, holding a bunch of long-stemmed roses.

Seeing him on her home ground, Veronica was struck again by how good-looking he was. She knew beyond a shadow of doubt that she wanted to look into his dear, kind face for the rest of her life. She took the roses from him and before she'd even put them in a vase, he was kissing her, and he just looked so... well, at home, in her kitchen, that in no time flat he'd been staying with her for a week.

V eronica took a sip of coffee and looked around. The dragonfly was still patrolling. So much had happened since her winter cruise.

Anna was a changed woman. Marriage really suited her, and she and Alex had given up the rented cottage and bought a house a few miles away. Anna was also showing some rather late nesting instincts... as she said, they had no time to lose!

As for Veronica, well... she could scarcely believe it. Here she was on the eve of her wedding. Two weddings in the family. She couldn't be happier.

And all because of a spot of rain. Ⓜ

Sun, Sea And Second Chances

The nightmare night had haunted her, but now her dreams would be much sweeter

By TESS NILAND KIMBER

ILLUSTRATIONS: ISTOCKPHOTO, MANDY DIXON

Sharp sunlight glinted off the turquoise sea which was hugged by a semi-circle of rocky, almost prehistoric cliffs. Hannah sighed. There was no doubt about it, Menorca was stunning.

"A glass of white wine, one of those pomadas everyone's talking about and a pina colada," drawled a very sunburned American lady.

"Coming right up," Hannah said, hoping there was enough fresh pineapple in the fridge for the pina colada.

Even with the breeze sighing across the Mediterranean and dressed in a white vest top and shorts, she was feeling seriously hot. Somehow ➤

53

the late afternoon sun crept under the canopy covering Chiringuitos, the beach bar she was managing for the summer.

"Are you OK?" she asked Pablo, the other bar tender, who was trying to restock the shelves with bottles of beer. "You need to take a break soon."

"I'm fine." He smiled, a light dancing in his blue eyes as he stacked the now empty crate behind the bar.

Even by Chiringuitos' standards they were busy. But why was she surprised? This was the height of Menorca's summer season and the bar was everything the owner had claimed. The location was beautiful – the view over the beach to die for. Other than a couple of rainy days, the weather had been perfect and the bar had a reputation for fair prices and a scrumptious menu – all the right ingredients for a successful business. It was all she'd dreamed when studying her travel and tourism degree.

Besides, being busy was the perfect antidote for a broken heart, she thought, mixing the lemonade and gin for the local favourite pomada.

Putting the drinks on a tray she took payment from the American lady before serving her next customer.

"A pint of…" The man suddenly stopped speaking. "Hannah?"

She looked up, straight into the light brown eyes of Ollie Redmond.

"Ollie! Umm … hi," she spluttered. "What … are you doing here?"

"Hey – hurry up – I'm dying of thirst while you two chat," shouted a tattooed man, standing behind Ollie.

"Sorry – what would you like, Ollie?"

"Two pints of cider and a diet coke, please."

She busied herself with his order, terribly aware of those gorgeous eyes watching her. She hadn't seen him since … her face flushed, remembering the last hugely embarrassing moment they'd shared.

"I'm on holiday with Aaron and Tom. Tom's getting married next month, so it's his last taste of freedom," Ollie laughed, counting out some euros. "Menorca's great but Aaron's moaning about the lack of night-life."

"There are a few clubs, but Menorca's more for families."

"He messed up the booking – thought we were going to Majorca not

Menorca," he raised his dark eyebrows. "Any recommendations?"

"Well, I'm usually too exhausted after a day here to worry..." she said, although the truth was, after their last meeting and the break-up of her romance with Ezra, she'd lost the confidence to hit the clubs. "I've heard there's some great places in Son Bou. Try them out..."

"I intend to," he said, holding her gaze. "Will I see you around later?"

"If you come back here then probably ... I'd better get on," she said, brutally aware the tattooed man was looking crosser by the minute. "Now sir, what can I get you?"

She took his food order while her head buzzed with thoughts of Ollie Redmond. She'd left England to escape men and her problems, yet Ollie had turned up here in Menorca. It was hardly a remote island but she

Being busy was the perfect anecdote for a broken heart

hadn't expected to run into someone she knew so early in her managership of the bar. So much for getting away from it all, hey!

The afternoon passed in a blur. While Hannah and Pablo were run off their feet, Ollie joined his friends at Chiringuitos' picnic tables, under the shade of the thatched umbrellas. She was intensely aware of him. But more than that, she burned with embarrassment, remembering their last meeting...

It had been Christmas and she'd been celebrating in Canterbury uni's bar after gaining a merit for her latest essay. She was sharing a bottle of wine with her friend Nadia when Ollie came into the bar with his friends.

"If you like Ollie, ask him out," Nadia had urged.

"Oh," Hannah had said. "I don't feel comfortable making the first move. You know... after..."

Nadia had rolled her brown eyes. "I know you've had problems but, come on, it's 2021 not 1921. Feminism, girl power – call it what you want – we women can take control these days, you know."

Empowered by both Nadia's words and the wine, Hannah had ➞

joined Ollie at the bar where he was chatting to his mates.

"Hi," she'd smiled.

"Hannah – hello. Good to see you," he'd smiled back.

He really was gorgeous, she thought, with light brown eyes, close cropped beard and dark hair. And he'd the body to match. Studying sports, he was super fit.

"Could I... umm... have a word?" Already her nerve was failing.

She glanced towards Nadia who mouthed, "Go on!"

"Sure," he said distractedly, not attempting to move away from his friends who'd stopped chatting to listen to them.

Ollie's rejection of her had made a big impact on her life decisions

She hesitated. This wasn't how she'd planned it. Why hadn't she asked to speak to him privately?

"Umm..." she could feel her face burning.

"It's OK – I don't bite." He laughed.

Feeling it would be more embarrassing not to speak than to ask him out, she blurted out, "I wondered... if... you'd like to come out with me one evening?"

There! She'd said it. She smiled, although her face felt weird as if her lips were stuck to her front teeth.

Ollie's own smile faded. "I'm sorry, Hannah. That's really kind of you to ask but I'm afraid..."

Despite his polite answer, all she could hear was NO! NO! NO!

"Don't worry – no problem. I was just asking. See you around, Ollie."

"Hannah – wait!" he called.

But she wasn't going to wait. Turning on her heel, she rushed back to Nadia. Why had she listened to her?

"I'm going," she said, grabbing her coat.

"Wait!" Nadia called.

But Hannah didn't intend spending another second in the busy bar. She was marching down the street, in the cold night air, by the time Nadia caught up with her.

"Where are you going?" Nadia gasped, clutching Hannah's arm.

"Home!"

"Why? What happened?"

Hannah stopped walking. "It was so embarrassing! Ollie said no!"

"Why?"

"Never said... It was awful. I'm never doing that again."

As they walked back to the house they shared with two other students, Nadia offered several reasons for his response.

But all Hannah could think was that Ollie, whom she'd lusted after for weeks, had said no, in front of his friends, in the busy union bar.

She'd be a laughing stock! She wasn't like Nadia who oozed confidence. Her teenaged years had been hard. She'd struggled with self-esteem, especially since...

Now as Hannah collected glasses from the tables, she thought how much that December evening had impacted her.

If she hadn't felt so mortified she'd probably never have said yes when Ezra asked her out the following week. Ezra was the total opposite to Ollie – loud, pushy, confident. Up for a laugh, he seemed the perfect remedy for her hurt pride.

The sun set in an orangey glow over the Mediterranean. All around couples, arms wrapped around each other, wandered along the beach. Was it only Hannah who was alone?

Hannah had always loved Menorca, spending most of her childhood holidays here. Quieter than mainland Spain, she and her sister Michelle had made the most of windsurfing, sailing and waterskiing in the crystal-clear water. So, when she'd had the idea of running her own beach bar, Menorca was the obvious choice.

"You sure, Hannah?" her mum had asked when she'd revealed her plans. "It'll be great experience but..."

Hannah understood her mum's hesitation. She'd always lacked Michelle's confidence. When Hannah had developed an eating disorder at secondary school, her self-esteem had nose-dived. Early intervention and therapy helped her overcome her eating issues but her ➜

confidence had nevertheless remained on a permanent diet.

"You should be so proud of yourself," Michelle used to say, hugging her. "Think how much you've achieved. You've battled your problems and won."

Michelle's support had helped her find the strength to study at uni but she still struggled with things other girls on her course achieved without thinking. Like asking guys out...

Working in Menorca was a big step and she'd made a success of it.

"You eating OK?" her mum would check when they Skyped.

"Oh yes." She'd laugh. "It's gorgeous food here – fish, fruit, salads. Nothing I'd want to skip."

However, that night after seeing Ollie at Chiringuitos, she'd pushed her meal around her plate. It was the first time in almost two years she'd rejected her food.

Dating was a minefield. Ezra had proved a nightmare. At first, he'd been fun and even considered joining her in Menorca. Then he'd started messing her around – cancelling dates and if he did show, he was glued to his phone. When Nadia told her she'd seen him in town with another girl when he was supposed to be "revising," she hadn't been surprised.

However, this latest rejection hit her hard. After gaining her degree, she couldn't wait to leave for Menorca.

So far, the move had been positive. She loved the island and the super-friendly locals. But then Ollie had turned up and her feelings of worthlessness had returned with a vengeance.

She put down her knife and fork. Maybe her appetite would return when Ollie and his mates left.

The next day at Chiringuitos, Hannah checked constantly for signs of Ollie and his mates. When he, Tom and Aaron arrived in the afternoon, Hannah hissed to Pablo, "Please can you serve that guy?"

"But I thought you are friends?" Pablo smiled, his blue eyes twinkling.

"I know him – and we're not friends," she said, ducking behind the bar, pretending to check the stock.

When she thought the coast was clear she popped back up to serve other customers. She could feel Ollie watching her and once thought he'd waved but she'd studiously ignored him.

Later, she saw him walking over to the bar. Quickly she disappeared to the kitchen area to make up some food orders. Hoping he'd gone, she returned to the bar only to bump straight in to him.

"Hannah?" Ollie smiled.

Red-faced, she said. "Oh hi... Sorry. Didn't see you there."

"And I thought you were avoiding me... Look, can we chat?"

"Well, Pablo and I are very busy..."

"Later then. You must get a break?"

She glanced at Pablo who nodded for her to go.

"OK – I'll have a drink when I've cleared these orders."

He smiled. "I'll look forward to it. Introduce you to Tom and Aaron."

Hannah almost groaned. That's all she needed – getting to know two men who were at the union that evening and who almost certainly were laughing behind her back.

L ater, urged on by Pablo, Hannah took a cold drink and went to sit with Ollie. Luckily Tom and Aaron had gone swimming.

"Great to see you again, Hannah...

She could feel Ollie watching her but studiously ignored him

Menorca mightn't have much nightlife but it's growing on us. Lovely scenery and we visited the Cathedral Ciudadela yesterday. Gorgeous."

Hannah was surprised. She'd imagined they'd only be interested in the pool and bars.

"Isn't it! I went last month for the first time. It's pristine and the stained glass windows are fab."

"Yes, I thought it was a modern church as the lines were so clean." She smiled and sipped her drink.

"Look, Hannah, I want to apologise. Last time we met... at uni..."

She stood up. "Really – it's OK. It was my fault... Look, I must get back. Pablo... it's busy."

Her words tumbling, she turned and rushed back to the bar. ➔

"You OK?" Pablo asked, obviously concerned.

"Yes," she said, shaking. "But if that man asks to speak to me again, tell him I'm busy."

"He not hurt you?"

"Oh no. Nothing like that. I just don't want to talk to him."

Later Hannah handed over the bar to Camila. It had been a long day. She was tired but before she could head to her apartment she must go shopping. She'd only just got through the doors when she saw Ollie.

"Hello again!"

Why hadn't she gone straight home? She groaned.

"It's becoming a habit," he said, catching her hand. "You running off when we speak."

She glanced down. "Sorry Ollie, it's just... I feel so... so embarrassed whenever I see you."

"Don't be!" He laughed. "Look – we can't chat here. There's a coffee shop across the road. Meet me when you've finished shopping?"

"OK." She sighed.

"And no running off this time!"

"No, I promise." She smiled.

"I owe you an apology. I upset you but I didn't mean to"

Hannah could hardly concentrate on her list but once through the check-out, she made her way to Café Hola. The round tables had glass tops and were surrounded by purple painted chairs. She soon saw Ollie.

"What would you like?" he asked.

"Frappe would be great."

As he queued, she thought again how lovely he was. If only he'd said yes when she'd asked him out.

He returned with two cups.

"Look, I owe you an apology. I upset you in the union that evening, but I didn't mean to."

"It was my fault. I shouldn't have asked you out. It's not my style."

He sipped his cappuccino. "Well, I was flattered. It's not every day a man's asked out by a beautiful girl."

Her face burned at his compliment. "My friend... she knew I liked you and urged me to ask you. Like I say – it's not what I do, normally."

"I didn't say no because I didn't like you," he said, his light brown eyes locked into hers.

Hannah tingled. He really was so kind, trying to make her feel better. And it was working.

"I said no because I already had a girlfriend... I'd have explained but you didn't give me a chance."

She was shocked. "But I... I never saw you with a girl around uni."

"I knew Chloe from school. She didn't go to uni. She stayed in our old hometown."

Relief flooded her. He'd rightly turned her down because he had a serious girlfriend, not because he wasn't attracted to her.

"I thought we'd be together forever... but we were with each other for just two years."

"Were?" she said, tentatively.

"Yes... we split up at Easter. Being at uni – sadly, we grew apart."

"I'm sorry," she said, quietly. "For you and for Chloe, and also for asking you out. I'd never have dreamed of doing so if I'd known you weren't single. I'm sorry."

Ollie smiled. "Don't be... The next guy you ask will be very lucky."

"No way! I'll wait to be asked next time."

"Well, in that case," he said, reaching for her hand. "How about having dinner with me tonight?"

She smiled. "Don't feel you have to ask me."

"I'm asking because I want to. If I'd been single, I'd have jumped at the chance of a date with you."

"Really?" she said, smiling into his gorgeous eyes.

"Yes – really. Now where's the best place to eat round here?"

Slowly she felt her appetite returning – for food... and for life.

Holiday For One

She'd hoped for an escape, but what was it, exactly, that she was trying to escape?

By ISABELLE BROOM

Anthea settled down in her deckchair and let out a long, contented sigh. She had made it. She was in Portugal, on a beach, with sand between her toes and sunshine warm as toast on her cheeks. It was beautiful, it was serene and, best of all, she was free to enjoy it alone.

When Anthea's husband Phil had suggested she take some time away to rest and recuperate after the – he had punctuated the phrase with a polite cough – "recent turmoil", she had initially refused. She couldn't simply swan off and leave him and the kids back in Surrey, could she?

As it turned out, she very much could.

Anthea opened the novel she had been trying and failing to read since Charlie and Maeve were born, sixteen and thirteen years ago respectively, and shuffled down until her bottom was in an optimum position of comfort. A lazy breeze danced in from across the water and chased a few errant strands of hair across her cheeks, a soft whisper from Mother Nature herself, telling Anthea parent-to-parent that this was her time, that she had earned it, that it was perfectly acceptable to enjoy the moment, the solitude, the peace and quiet...

"Excuse me, love – alright if I pitch up here?"

Anthea jumped, her novel dropping into her lap. The woman who'd just appeared beside her was sporting an enormous UFO-shaped hat that was entirely blocking out the sun, and Anthea blinked furiously as her eyes readjusted.

"Of course." She gestured with a hand. "Feel free."

"Nice spot this," the woman said happily, unfolding her own deckchair and heaving a gargantuan striped bag down from her shoulder. From this she extracted a rolled-up towel, sun lotion, three magazines, a bottle of Coke, bright-pink flip-flops and a small cushion.

"Have to be careful with my back," she explained, wincing as she lowered herself into the seat. "Never been the same since my Kyle was born. Over ten pounds on the scales he was – head as big as a watermelon."

Anthea wrinkled up her nose in a mixture of sympathy and horror. She had thought Charlie big at eight pounds three ounces – over ten was unimaginable.

"Golly," she replied, pushing the appalling image of a baby with a melon instead of a head from her mind. "Poor you."

"You got any kids?" the woman went on, slathering cream across her chest. She was fair haired but already deeply tanned, and the oil she was using had an SPF of just four. Anthea had carefully applied factor fifty to every exposed area of skin, then put a kaftan on over her swimsuit for good measure.

"Two," Anthea said, detailing their names and ages.

→

"Five," the woman replied. "Four lads and a lass, and she's a right thorn in my side."

Kath, as she now introduced herself, then continued with a groan, "I was never as angsty as her when I was a nipper. Nowadays it's all, "so and so hasn't tagged me in her Tik Tok' and "this, that, the other hasn't watched my Insta story'. It's all gobbledegook to me. The boys are far more straightforward."

Anthea, who had confiscated her son's mobile phone after "the incident", merely nodded.

A flock of small birds had landed down by the shoreline and she strained to hear the heart-warming sound of their little chirps.

How had her boy so quickly gone from cherubic to troubled?

At home it was always so go-go-go: the bang of the porridge pot against the stovetop in the morning, the yelling up the stairs that the kids needed to get a wriggle on, the coffee machine whirring, Radio Four blathering, Skipper the dog barking as the post dropped through the letterbox, the slam of her car door, followed by the hum of traffic, the ping of the elevator, the ringing of her phone at the office, the chatter of colleagues...

If she was lucky, Anthea grabbed a solo half-hour in the tub after dinner, but even then there would be knocks at the door... Mum, where's my blue top? Mum, Skipper needs a pee. Mum, why are you ignoring me – have you drowned? Dad! Daaaaad! Mum's drowned!

She had hoped this week in the Algarve would be a chance to switch off from all that noise, from life, from the demands of being a working mother and, of course, from the "recent turmoil".

"You all right there, love?"

Kath was peering at her in mild concern.

"Sorry," Anthea shook her head. "I was miles away," she added, wishing as she said it that she actually was. Kath seemed nice enough, but she was chatty. Very chatty. Anthea suppressed a yawn.

"I get it." Kath held up both hands. "You're wanting a nice nap and then along I come with my big old gob and disturb you. Say no more."

"No, honestly, it's fine," began Anthea.

"Pretend I'm not really here," Kath stage whispered. "I won't say another word."

Smiling in defeat, Anthea leant back against her chair and closed her eyes, listening to the gentle roar of the waves. Faint notes of music were drifting down from the beach bar, and from somewhere in the distance, she could hear the tap-tap of a ball against a bat. The warmth eased its way into her limbs, feeling so much like the expert hands of a masseuse as it soothed and melted away all of her stress and tension.

She still could not quite believe he had done it. Not her boy – not her little Charlie. How had he gone from being cherubic to troubled so quickly? Had she taught him nothing? Had her and Phil's example really been so bad?

"You really shouldn't do that."

Anthea opened one eye. "Pardon?"

"You were frowning – in your sleep, like," Kath said gravely. "Thought it better I wake you than watch you gain a wrinkle."

"Oh, I wasn't asleep," Anthea replied, choosing not to add that chance would be a fine thing.

"That book any good?" Kath went on, unperturbed.

"Honestly?" Anthea held it up. "I have no idea. I bought it to read when I was on maternity leave and have yet to start the first chapter."

Kath laughed at that, sounding so much like a braying donkey that Anthea found herself joining in.

"You have to giggle, don't you?" spluttered Kath. "It's either that or cry, and I think if I started, I might never stop."

Anthea was reminded of herself only a few weeks ago, knocked sideways with disappointment, weeping herself to sleep beside a snoring Phil. Her husband had laughed when he heard what Charlie had done – laughed!

"However do you cope with five?" she asked Kath. "You must have to be very strict." ➙

Kath guffawed. "Nah, gave up on all that years ago. My lot are basically feral. The boys refuse to clean their rooms – I found a family of mice in my eldest's last time I went to pick up his washing – and my Lucy's no bleedin' better. There's not a surface of my house not smeared with make-up, and Kyle hides his bogies behind my sofa cushions!"

Anthea pictured crusty curls on her white Habitat couch and shuddered.

"I'd ground them all," Kath went on, "But then the bleeders would be in the house with me all the time, and that really would drive me mad. I mean, us mums need our alone time, don't we? A bit of peace and quiet, away from all the demands."

Anthea almost choked on the irony of the situation.

"The worst was when Big Tone – he's my second-eldest – got arrested for trying to pinch a load of top shelf mags from the newsagent. Being big, you see, he could reach the top shelf by the age of twelve."

"Arrested?" This time Anthea really did choke.

"Yeah." Kath was nonplussed. "He said his mates dared him, but that's no excuse, is it? I couldn't look the woman that runs the joint in the eye for years after that."

A beach ball bounced towards them at speed, but while Anthea cringed in her seat, Kath simply stretched out a foot and booted it hard in the opposite direction.

"Then again," she mused. "There's no real harm in a bit of natural curiosity. Boys will be boys and all that, right?'

Anthea reddened as she recalled, once again, the topless images she had discovered on her son Charlie's phone. Seeing them there had felt to Anthea like taking a bullet to the chest at the time, but could she have overreacted?

"I mean," Kath was saying, "I pretended I was cross with him, of course, but behind the scenes, me and the other half were killing ourselves laughing about it."

Anthea nodded in an imitation of agreement, before gazing away towards the horizon. She found that if she focused hard enough on that quivering blue line, where the gentle folds of the sea met the smooth cobalt canvas of the sky, she could almost zone out all other noise.

"Will you watch my chair, please?" she said, suddenly and quickly getting to her feet.

"Course." Kath tossed a couple of her magazines into the vacated seat. Anthea thought she heard her call out something else as she hurried away, but she didn't look back, didn't stop until she had reached the beach taverna, connected her phone to the Wi-Fi, and pressed the button to make a FaceTime call.

Phil answered on the third ring.

"Hello, love. Oh, you're at the beach – that's great. How are you? Feeling better for having escaped?"

Had she simply over reacted? "Boys will be boys, right?"

"I'll tell you all about it in a minute," Anthea promised. "But first, can you put Charlie on? Oh, and get Maeve, too."

"You want the kids?" Her husband was clearly bemused. "But you only saw them yesterday."

"I know.' Anthea smiled, tears in her eyes now as she realised how ridiculous she'd been, how reactionary. How much she had made the situation with Charlie about herself, rather than him. "But I miss them," she cried. "I miss them so much. I miss you all so much."

"Well, then, if that's the case," Phil said, raising a single eyebrow. "Why don't I book us a flight so we can come out and join you? I can easily move some stuff around at work. How would you like that?"

Anthea turned and stared out at golden-caster sand peppered with colourful beach umbrellas, at the deckchair she had set up and the novel she had abandoned, yet again, on the floor beside it.

She'd assumed getting away would make her feel more like her old pre-motherhood self, but all it had done was remind her that her she preferred her new self far more.

"I think," she said, giving in to a smile as bright as sunlight on water, "I would like that very much." (MW)

Call Of
The Wild

Tired of life revolving around screens, Sam tried to show his family a different way…

By LISA ALLEN

Sam gazed around the lounge at the three zombies he shared his home with. His son, Charlie, currently mid-battle with an alien. His daughter, Matilda, staring at a picture of her own face with computer generated cat ears and cat nose. And his wife, Lucy, who was being hypnotised by some people in an East End boozer who kept shouting "Get outta maah pub!"

Sam sighed.

School holiday season was approaching and it was making him feel nostalgic. He loved school holidays when he was a boy. Weekends camping in the New Forest with his dad, summer breaks sailing their old dinghy along the shallows of the Devon coastline, or exploring rock-pools of Cornish coves.

When had everything changed? The last time the four of them had a family day out, Matilda announced her social media life was about to go into crisis because she couldn't get a 4G signal.

He and Lucy had both booked a week off work to coincide with the kids' school holidays, and he had just decided exactly how they were going to spend it.

"We're going away on holiday next week," Sam announced brightly.

Three heads popped up like meerkats, staring at him in surprise.

"To Disneyland?" asked Charlie, excitement in his voice.

Sam nearly choked on his coffee. "No," he spluttered. "Not to Disneyland. Better actually – we're going camping."

A groan rumbled around the lounge like a dinosaur in pain.

"I am not going camping." Matilda folded her arms in defiance. She'd already made plans for a shopping trip with her friends.

"James in my class, his parents are taking him to the Maldives for the holidays. I want to go to the Maldives," Charlie whined.

Matilda scoffed. "You don't even know where the Maldives are."

"Yes I do – because I'm the clever one in the family." He pulled a face at her.

Sam scowled. "Do James's parents have room for one more?"

Charlie pondered. "Doubt it – he's got quite an extended family." →

"Looks like you're going camping with us then."

Lucy had remained unusually quiet up to this point. "Sam, we haven't got a tent. Tents are very expensive." She still had one eye on the Queen Vic's landlord.

"We'll borrow my brother's tent." Sam rubbed his hands together triumphantly. "This is going to be our best holiday yet. You'll see!"

"Wouldn't be difficult. We only ever go to Auntie Holly's house. And it always rains," mumbled Matilda, as three pairs of eyes went back to fighting aliens, looking at the face of a cat-girl, and watching two women wearing leopard print leggings have a scrap.

They were five days into their family holiday. Sam had driven them up to the Lake District in their decrepit estate car, camping equipment squeezed into every available space, suitcases rattling on the roof-rack.

With much cajoling, ultimatums, and tantrums that were worthy of an acting award, Sam had managed to awaken the "outdoor adventurers" in his wife and children. They'd spent the past few days begrudgingly exploring the breathtaking mountain trails, cycling along tranquil country lanes, and – oh yes – embracing the misfortune of having to walk through a field of cows to get to the toilets in the middle of the night!

Despite all this, as Sam sat in his foldable camping chair, a kettle bubbling away on the gas stove, he still didn't feel they'd quite entered into the spirit of a good old-fashioned camping holiday. He gazed at their little group clustered by their tent among green fields, and felt disappointed. Charlie was lost in battle on his handheld games console, Matilda swiped her finger across her electronic tablet, and Lucy had her nose buried in a Kindle. They were together, but still all doing their own things.

"How about a boat trip on the lake this afternoon?" His bright, hopeful voice drowned out the whistling of the kettle.

Matilda briefly glanced up. "No. Way. It's bad enough you dragged us through a holiday time-warp back to 1940, just so you can relive your youth. I'm not going to risk drowning as well."

Sam gasped. "1940? I'm not that old!"

Lucy peeked over her book, a twinkle in her eye. "You're fifty this year, dear."

Sam glared at her.

"Charlie, what about you? Fancy being my captain's mate on the high seas?"

Charlie groaned, flinging his games console to the ground. "Might as well, the zombies have crushed my planet."

Sam knew exactly how he felt.

Two hours later, the four of them were sailing across Lake Windermere. The sun glistened on the ripples, the mountains either side stretched up into a cerulean sky, and the light breeze pushed the billowing white sails of their boat back to the jetty, Sam at the helm.

"This is so cool, Dad," Charlie's face tilted skywards mirroring the sun's beaming smile. "I can't believe I've never been sailing before."

Sam glanced over his shoulder, catching the relaxed and happy grin on his wife's face, the worries of daily life washing away. "I'm glad you're enjoying it, Charlie. I used to go sailing with my dad all the time when I was your age."

It's bad enough you dragged us through a holiday time warp to 1940

"Can I steer the boat, Dad?" Matilda grabbed the helm with her usual teenage sense of entitlement, but this time Sam didn't mind one bit. His heart filled with pride. Finally, a part of the holiday they were all enjoying.

And not a smartphone, games console, or TV screen in sight.

"Course you can, love. Watch the sail as we turn, though." He looked around the boat, ensuring the safety of his fellow adventurers. "Everyone, when I say so, we all need to – "

"Duck!" shouted Lucy, panic crashing into her face as the sail winged from one side of the boat to the other, knocking Sam straight overboard!

"Man overboard!" shouted Charlie, almost gleefully.   →

Three sets of eyes stared anxiously over the side of the boat.

Suddenly Sam's life-jacket floated him round port side of the vessel, his hands and legs flapping about like a duck.

"Oh, thank goodness!" Lucy reached down her arm for him to cling on to. "Are you OK? You look like you're in shock."

Sam burst out laughing so uncontrollably he was making waves against the boat. Suddenly nothing seemed to matter anymore – he'd done it. The sailing had brought them all back together again. Even if it had ended with him going for an unexpected, and very cold, swim.

Matilda and Charlie exchanged looks. "Do you think he's suffering from hypothermia?"

I just wanted you to enjoy the kind of holidays that I used to have

"Help me pull him back into the boat," instructed Lucy. "Mind you don't fall in as well. Charlie, can you drive? Let's get him back ashore."

"Sail, Mum. It's sail a boat," Charlie corrected, rolling his eyes.

"Are you OK sweetheart?" Lucy's eyes met Sam's as he sat next to her, shivering, covered in lake-water debris.

Sam grinned. "Never been better. I've got my family, we're on holiday, and I've even managed to wean you all off your gadgets – if only for a couple of hours. What more could I ask for?"

Lucy slid her arms around his shoulders and gave him a gentle kiss on the cheek. "We love you, Sam, I hope you know that, even if we don't always show it. If anything ever happened to you, I don't know what we'd do."

Sam's eyes met Lucy's, and he rested his hand on hers. "You lot are my world, Lucy. I don't plan on going anywhere just yet."

They sat in a row on the wall outside the campsite's takeaway, Sam with a towel around his shoulders, as they all devoured their way through boxes of fish and chips.

"Have you had enough of camping yet, darling?" Lucy sceptically arched an eyebrow, while Matilda and Charlie both looked at their dad and giggled.

Sam stuffed a chip in his mouth, ignoring them. "I just wanted to show you that life doesn't have to revolve around technology all the time. I wanted you to enjoy the holidays I used to love."

"And we have." Lucy rested her hand on his arm. "It's been lovely to get away."

Sam smiled.

"Yeah Dad, it hasn't been that bad," added Matilda – almost brightly, he thought.

"That's teenager code for she's had a good holiday," whispered Lucy.

Sam grinned. "And what about you, Charlie?"

Charlie looked up. "I'd say sailing's been the best so far. It was sooo funny when you fell in the water!"

Matilda snorted.

Sam rolled his eyes, wryly. "Glad to have been so entertaining."

"So, where to for holidays next year, kids?" asked Lucy with anticipation.

"I hear Disney's very nice," offered Charlie, a flicker of hope in his little face. "Apparently they've got this new ride and it's just like literally being in a computer game."

Lucy and Matilda burst out laughing.

"I tried," sighed Sam, shaking his head in exasperation. "You can't say I didn't try…" Ⓜ

Paris On A Shoestring

They were going to separate universities… could their love withstand the distance?

By TESS NILAND KIMBER

Livvy watched in awe as the artists worked on their paintings in the famous Artists Square in Montmartre. As an art student there was no better buzz than being in the very spot where Degas and Matisse had once worked.

"Isn't this wonderful?" she said to Noah, squeezing his hand.

"Well, it's wonderful being here with you," he said, lifting the brim of her floppy straw hat to kiss her. "But I'm not sure if seeing Paris on such a tight budget works."

As they moved away from the artists, she tried to reassure him. "It doesn't matter. We're here. Together."

And it didn't matter. Warm enough for shorts, the weather was fantastic, the atmosphere intoxicating, and she was in Paris with the man she loved.

Let's go to Paris," Noah had said, over lunch break a few weeks ago. Saving money for uni, they'd taken summer jobs at the local supermarket.

"Can we afford it?" she frowned.

"No," he'd grinned, pushing a hand through his dark hair. "But it'll be the perfect end to the summer."

End. The word chilled Livvy, reminding her they'd soon be apart. Of course, she was looking forward to her art course at Bournemouth uni but Noah would be miles away, studying biochemistry in Nottingham.

Livvy couldn't remember a time without him. A childhood friendship had blossomed into a teenage romance and now they were madly in love.

"Boring," her best friend Martha teased. "Join Tinder when you go to uni. Find someone new."

"No way," Livvy had smiled.

There was only one man for her and that was Noah. She only hoped he felt the same…

"We'll FaceTime at uni. And we'll be home for the holidays. It won't be so bad," he'd consoled.

But worried the distance would spell the end of their relationship, she was thrilled when he suggested the Paris trip.

"We've worked hard this summer. Let's enjoy a break together before uni."

"But isn't Paris expensive?" Livvy frowned.

"Where isn't?" he'd smiled. "I'll research it. Do it on the cheap."

She'd been sceptical but they travelled by coach – an arduous seven-and-a-half-hour journey – and booked a clean but basic hostel.

All they forgot was enough spending money…

→

If only we had more cash," Noah complained.

She curled her arms around his waist. "It doesn't matter. It's magical – being here with you."

"Yes, but I wanted to show you the sights – Champs Elysees, the Eiffel Tower, Notre Dame..."

"Don't worry – we'll still see them. We can stand outside. Take photos."

He smiled at her enthusiasm although she felt a pang when the modest entrance fee to Le Louvre exceeded their funds.

"Another time, hey?" she sighed.

So, they spent the afternoon travelling around the city, visiting numerous attractions.

"It's like a pedestrian coach tour," she smiled.

The Eiffel Tower stood against a sunset-painted pink and gold sky

"Well, we've seen almost everything even if we have had to stand outside like stalkers."

Livvy laughed but didn't feel they'd missed out. It was romantic walking through the busy arrondissements and parks, soaking up the atmosphere, and experiencing the authentic Paris together.

But, during the afternoon, wandering hand-in-hand along the banks of the river Seine, Noah still complained they weren't having the full Paris experience.

"We ought to be sailing the river in a glass bottomed boat."

"One day."

"Maybe," he said, sadly.

Gorgeous smells drifted from the restaurants and food stalls. Hungry, he suggested they ate.

"We haven't enough money to dine in a bistro," she admitted, "so let's go to a boulangerie."

Pooling their funds, they bought warm crusty baguettes, ham, cheese and salad.

"Where shall we eat? In the park?"

"No," she said excitedly. "I have an idea. Come on."

"Where?"

She put a finger to her lips. "I'm not saying. It's a surprise."

By the time they reached her destination, where they bought coffee from a roadside stall, afternoon had slipped into early evening.

"Here we are," she said, as they sat down on the paving. "Place du Trocadero."

"Wow!" he said. "Look at that view."

The sunset had painted the sky with a pallet of blue, pink and gold. In the distance stood the majestic Eiffel Tower. In awe, they ate the delicious food. When they finished, they watched the last of the sun disappear.

"This is wonderful," Noah sighed.

"See – we don't have to have spend a fortune to enjoy Paris."

"No, but one day we'll come back – experience it properly. Stay at the best hotel. That's if you want to."

"Want to? Of course I do."

"Oh, thank God. I thought, once we're at uni, you'd finish with me. That's why I've been so upset that I couldn't treat you to everything while we're here."

Livvy laughed. "That's been my fear, too."

"Well, here's to next time," he said, bumping his paper coffee cup against hers.

Next time. It sounded magical, she thought, resting her head on his shoulder. They still had a future – together. She'd been so scared that somehow Noah would find Nottingham and uni life more exciting than dating her.

Being together like this in Paris, her fears melted away. He wanted to be with her just as much as she wanted to be with him. Somehow, during uni, they'd find a way to make it work. Whatever the distance... MW

Into The Sunshine

A minor accident, an over-reaction… can Melissa's daughter Rosie overcome it?

By PHOEBE MORGAN

The olive trees cast shadowy dapples on the stone flags, the heat baking the ground. Melissa moves her chair, just slightly, so that the sun remains on the back of her neck, warming the already-browning skin. She has always loved the sun – usually, her daughter laughs at her, tells her she is like a cat on a hot tin roof.

At sixteen, Rosie is more aware than Melissa ever was at her age – preoccupied with the damage the sun can inflict, choosing instead to slather herself in factor 30 sun-cream and sit in the shade, her dark head covered by the red splash of the large parasol that hangs over the table, like a web suspended above prey. She hasn't laughed on this holiday, not once.

They have been abroad for almost a week already, and Melissa can feel herself relaxing more and more every day, allowing the stresses of her life back at home to lessen, recede a little.

It's not that she can forget what has happened, no, but she is giving herself permission to not think about it every waking minute. What happened back in England is not her fault, after all – the doctors told her that again and again. An accident – could have happened to anyone.

It is not Rosie's fault either, and everyone she spoke to had said that the best thing for them both would be for them to get away for a while – escape, as it were. It is the summer holidays, after all, the schools are out for six weeks. They are very lucky that her neighbour Janine had

offered them the house in France, free of charge.

She is more grateful for the offer than her neighbour will ever know.

It had been Rosie's first babysitting job. Melissa had smiled at her daughter's excitement over it – the chance to earn money was intoxicating at that age. Growing up, Melissa had asked her to do odd jobs around the house, but never paid her for it, choosing instead to reward her in other ways – an hour of TV, a sleepover with a friend. As a single mother, Melissa counted every penny, and although she would never let Rosie know it, the fact was that spare change wasn't something she had lying around very often. All the money Melissa earned went straight into savings; she was careful, and it had served them well over the years.

The babysitting job had come through a friend of a friend – a Mum at the school gates had been desperate. Rosie had jumped at the chance, and Melissa hadn't seen the harm – she was always so good with children, and interested in them, too. Melissa imagined her ➤

growing up to follow in her own footsteps, becoming a teacher or perhaps a nursery worker. She was caring, smart, resourceful; the sight of her with kids always made Melissa proud. Rosie would come to meet Melissa from work sometimes, and before term started she would help Melissa decorate her Year Three classroom, stapling brightly coloured pictures to the walls, laying out pencil pots on the desks with extra precision.

So what happened certainly wasn't her daughter's fault, and everyone was clear on that. The toddler she'd been looking after that night, a sweet little boy named Alfie, had crawled out of his cot, falling and banging his head. Rosie's call to her mother had been hysterical, and Melissa had felt it – the gut-wrenching fear a mother feels at the sound of their own offspring crying. Alfie's mother had been phoned, of course. Despite the fact that a trip to the hospital had proven that Alfie was fine, his mother Louise had been vicious in her criticism of poor Rosie – so much so that Melissa had feared her daughter's easy confidence around children would vanish forever.

"She's just frightened," Janine next door had soothed Melissa a few nights later, "She's frightened that something like that could happen again. And Alfie's mother's just reacting in a primal way, that's all. Louise is probably annoyed with herself, deep down. She must know that it wasn't Rosie's fault."

Melissa has been waiting for a phone call from Louise. Even now, in France, she keeps checking her phone, though this afternoon she has promised herself to try not to. Rosie has apologised so many times, as has Melissa. They sent flowers and cards and explained until they are blue in the face. But Louise's attitude hasn't changed. The thought of her baby coming to harm has ignited something in her, despite the fact that the bump on Alfie's head, a minor injury in the first place, has long gone now.

Overhead, the sound of crickets is intense, like tiny violins rising to a crescendo and then falling, repetitive yet comforting. Melissa loves it here – the villa is beautiful; large pink flowers snake up the wrought-iron railings that surround the veranda, and at night the sky is so clear that she and Rosie can see stars. Back in London, the smoggy sky prevents this, and Melissa hopes somehow that the wide open space and the sunshine of the days will heal her daughter, release her from the guilt she so obviously still feels, even though Alfie is fine, even though the accident was not her fault.

It turned out the cot was faulty, a loose bar had allowed him to fall, and there was no way Rosie could ever have known. Louise had admitted this, but still somehow found a way to blame Melissa's daughter. "It's her own guilt, really," Janine insists.

Melissa looks now at her daughter, at her bent head, the way her limbs seem to fold in on one another in the deckchair. She is ostensibly reading a book, but how Melissa wishes she could make her laugh, bring her back to life. Perhaps tonight she will try harder – she has bought some seabass from the little market at

> Louise had been vicious in her blaming of Rosie for the accident

the bottom of the hill, cheaper out here than back in London. She will cook it for them both, open a bottle of wine perhaps, let Rosie have a small glass. Her daughter deserves to relax.

Melissa takes a drink of water from the bottle at her side, enjoying the cool sensation in her throat. It is so hot here, as though the sun could burn away their worries. She can but wish.

"Mum," her daughter calls out to her from where she is sat reading, "The phone. The phone's ringing."

Distracted by the heat and the crickets, Melissa hasn't noticed but Rosie is right – her mobile is vibrating where she has left it beside the sparkling blue swimming pool, laying beside her discarded, wide-brimmed hat. She gets to her feet, the stones boiling under her tread, and presses the phone to her ear.

"Melissa?"

The voice is unfamiliar at first, and then in a rush she realises – it is Louise. Alfie's mother. She has been hoping to hear from her for all ➔

these weeks now, that her voice on the end of the line feels odd, surprising, as though Melissa has conjured it up. A genie, with only one wish.

"It's Louise," the other woman says, "I'm just ringing to…"

Her voice tails off. Melissa can feel her daughter's eyes on her; she will be feeling anxious, wondering who is on the phone. Who it is that has called them on holiday with something, it seems, that can't wait.

"I wanted to apologise." Louise's words come out in a hot rush, and Melissa feels a floating sensation, as if she has risen up above the olive trees and is looking down on herself, hovering by the pool, the phone clutched to her ear. The plastic is hot against her head, she realises, and her hands are slippery with sweat.

> Melissa is determined that she will find a way to thank her

"I've been unfair to you, to Rosie," Louise says, "I'm sorry, Mel. I was so… so shocked by Alfie being hurt, that I couldn't… I needed someone to blame."

"Alfie's not hurt;" Melissa says, very quietly, almost under her breath, but Louise seems to hear her.

"No," she says, softly, "No. He's not, and I was wrong to blame your daughter. I'm so sorry, Melissa. Really, I am. And I'm sorry it's taken me so long to admit it."

There is a small silence. Melissa can feel the thrum of her heart in her ears. Rosie is gesturing to her, palms spread wide, wanting to know what is being said. Melissa finds her voice.

"Thank you, Louise," she says gently, "Thank you for ringing."

She hangs up, places the phone down on her sun lounger. The light through the olive trees spills over it. She could turn it off, now. They have got what they wanted, they can relax, untroubled by the outside world, in this beautiful setting – a proper holiday, like they haven't had for years. They haven't been able to afford one, and so Janine's generosity is appreciated more than words can say. Melissa will find a way to thank her, when they return home in a few days' time. She is determined to.

"That was Louise," she tells Rosie, hesitantly, unsure of how her daughter will react, "She says she's sorry, and she was wrong to blame you."

It is as though someone has turned on a switch – the relief that washes over her daughter's face is like a drug to Melissa, a happy, warm buzz spreads through her limbs as she watches Rosie relax – she can almost see the moment her lovely girl decides to forgive herself. She wants to laugh with joy.

"It's OK now," she tells Rosie, "It's OK."

Her daughter is smiling, a wide, open smile, showing all her teeth. She is so beautiful when she smiles – well, to Melissa, she is always gorgeous, but since the incident she has been permanently cast in shadow, her face marked by stress, by misplaced guilt. It is wonderful to see that disappear.

"Oh," she says, thickly, her sunglasses down over her eyes, little mirrors that reflect Melissa back at herself. "Oh. That's good. I'm glad."

"Come here," Melissa says, and she opens out her arms to her daughter, feels the lithe, slim limbs of her teenager wrap around her own. They stand together, illuminated in the sunshine, united in relief.

That evening, Rosie tells her mother that she will apply for a childcare qualification next year. She has wanted to for months, she says, but of late has thought that she should not, that somehow she doesn't deserve to.

"But that's wonderful," Melissa tells her, "Of course you should. You'll be brilliant."

"Thanks, Mum," Rosie says softly, and Melissa smiles at her, raises her wine glass aloft into the darkening blue sky.

The air around them is velvety and warm. In the morning, the sun will rise again, and together, they will sit in it.

There will be no more shade. 🅜🅦

Take A Chance On Me

Tom wasn't part of the plan… but maybe he could help Lani with finding answers

By SANDRA BANCROFT

Lani read the last page of her novel, snapped it shut and laid it down on the table in front of her.

"Good book?"

She swivelled her head in the direction of the voice. A man sat alone at the next table but one, an espresso cup and newspaper in front of him.

"My apologies," he continued, when she didn't reply. "I didn't mean to disturb you. It's just that you seemed so completely engrossed in your book that I assumed it must be a real 'page-turner'."

He made imaginary apostrophes with his fingers.

"No," she said, finally. "You're not disturbing me, and yes, it was good, a murder mystery."

In truth she had simply grabbed it as an afterthought, a last-minute purchase at the airport.

"I'm just surprised to hear an American accent," she added.

"I'm based here." At her questioning look, he explained, "Over at the American naval base. I'm an engineer."

He stood up, scraping his chair on the stone pavement and came towards her, hand extended.

"Tom."

She hesitated slightly before shaking his proffered hand and returning his smile.

"Lorraine – but everyone calls me Lani."

"Do you mind if I join you? I feel silly shouting across two tables."

"Not at all."

Lani answered with an instinctive politeness but wasn't at all sure whether she actually minded or not. She had flown to Spain to escape love and its inevitable heartbreak. Being hit on by a guy – even if he was a tall, dark and handsome cliché – was absolutely the last thing on her itinerary.

Before she could analyse her feelings further, Tom had fetched his newspaper and cup and sat down at her table, choosing the only chair in direct sunlight.

Lani remained in the shade. Even in February, the morning temperature rose quickly and the mercury had already reached the ➞

high teens. She was loath to let her pale winter skin be too shocked by the Spanish sun and was exposing it gradually.

He noted her empty cup.

"I'll order us more drinks."

"Coffee, please. White."

Tom summoned the waiter.

"Dos cafes, por favour. Un negro y otro con la leche."

"Very smooth," she commented, reluctantly impressed. "I generally follow the line that us Brits and Americans expect everyone else to speak English."

"Yes, we are a lazy lot, aren't we? But I'm trying to learn the language." Tom smiled, displaying even white teeth. "This is me on a normal day off. Drinking coffee and," pointing to the newspaper, "using the local rag to practise my Spanish." He threw her a mischievous grin. "And sometimes, as a treat, I chat up pretty brunette English girls as well."

He would find out she was battle hardened against men like him

"Would that be meant as a treat for them or for you?"

He chuckled, appreciatively.

"Pretty and smart."

Before she could think of another witty response their coffees arrived. While Tom chatted to the waiter, she took the opportunity to scrutinise him from under her eyelashes.

Short hair, brown eyes, straight nose and a wide mouth. His arms gesticulated wildly as he spoke with an easy charm to the waiter in what sounded to Lani like fluent Spanish.

He had long fingers, nails cut very short, and perfect half-moon cuticles. His skin was tanned, evidence of many hours spent under a hot sun.

He was certainly not backward in coming forward, either, as her gran would say. Well – he would soon find out that she was battle-hardened against men like him, who oozed wicked charm and sex appeal.

Whatever Tom was saying to the waiter brought forth guffaws of laughter that continued as the old man disappeared back into the cool darkness of the café.

"Soccer," Tom told her. "I've become addicted to the sport since I moved to Spain last year."

Lani nodded and took a sip of her coffee to hide a smile. She found his use of the word "soccer" rather than "football" quite sweet.

"So what brings you to Cadiz?"

"A last-minute break."

Hmmm. That was an understatement if ever there was one, she thought wryly.

"Alone?"

"Yes."

"Aha," he said leaning back in his chair and staring at her, eyes narrowed. "So now I have a mystery to solve: *The Case of the Beautiful Girl Alone in Cadiz so soon after Valentine's Day*. And I get three guesses to crack it."

"There's no mystery –" she began, but he waved her to silence.

"You're a royal princess in disguise experiencing a slice of life with us commoners?"

She shook her head, joining in his game. She wasn't going to fall for him, but that didn't mean she couldn't enjoy his company for the short while she had.

"You're a secret agent whose mission is to seduce secrets out of me."

"I didn't notice you – and, anyway, you spoke to me first."

"Ah, yes, but you knew it was my favourite café and that I wouldn't be able to resist you."

She raised her eyebrows in disbelief.

He stretched out and took her right hand, his fingers following the lines on her palm. His touch, though light, made her skin tingle.

"That leaves only one explanation." She held her breath. "It's fate."

For a moment Lani stared at him like a mesmerised rabbit. She found she wanted to believe him. But the next moment a trace of ➤

recent pain stabbed her and she quickly locked the lines of her defence back into place.

She tugged at her hand and he released it instantly.

"Nothing so exciting," she said briskly. "I just needed a bit of me-time."

"And what have you been doing with this me-time?"

She was grateful that he went with the flow of her conversation. The awkward moment had passed and the atmosphere between them was easy once again.

"For the first two days, I lay by the pool under a huge umbrella and slept. Day Three, here I am. Refreshed and keen to explore."

"And fortunately for you, you've found yourself an English-speaking guide who can show you the main tourist sites, keep you entertained and buy you the best lunch in Cadiz."

"How can I refuse?"

"What are we waiting for? Grab onto your hat and let's get exploring."

They walked along the old, narrow streets until finally one opened into a large square.

"This is Plaza de San Juan de Dios."

"It's beautiful," Lani said, looking around at the impressive buildings.

People filled the many cafés while others sat on the steps of the large monument that dominated the centre of the square. Children played in the fountains, shrieking in delight as they splashed under sprays of water that sparkled in the sunlight.

Grabbing her mobile from her bag, Lani clicked away, concentrating on light and perspective.

Tom appeared at her shoulder, handing her an ice cream cone. They headed towards the port where they stood in silence and looked across the glittering sea.

A catamaran sailed past.

"I wonder where it's going."

"Across the bay to Rota, where I share a flat with two marines."

"Is it pretty?" she asked.

"Very pretty. Head across tomorrow and I'll show you around."

"I'm afraid I can't. I'm flying home tomorrow."

"But you just got here."

"I know. I just… I just needed a couple of days to think things through and find some answers."

A coldness touched her hand. She glanced down to see little streams of ice cream melting between her fingers.

"If we've only one day to see the sights, we'd better get cracking. Do you need a handkerchief?" Tom asked, as she licked each of her fingers individually.

The soporific bubbling of waterfalls surrounded them

She shook her head, producing a packet of wet tissues with a triumphant "Ta-ra."

"Do you want to talk about it? I've been told I'm a good listener."

"I don't think so. But thanks anyway."

"If you change your mind, just holler," he said.

They strolled along Alameda Apodaca promenade. Tom tapped his chest.

"I'm just your regular guy next door. No exciting mystery. You could say, an open book."

His mock-serious expression made her laugh.

"Born and raised in Seattle, Washington, only son of Mr and Mrs T R Watts, majored in engineering, joined the Navy and here I am."

They arrived at Parque Genoves and sat on a bench.

"You know I love soccer; also Bob Dylan, *Star Trek* and Snoopy. And, well, that's all there is to know about me."

"Don't believe you."

"Stick around and see if it's true."

She leaned back and closed her eyes to avoid answering him.

The soporific bubbling of waterfalls surrounded them and →

parrots screeched in the treetops, giving a sense of sitting in a tropical jungle.

"I can't believe I'll be shivering back home tomorrow," she murmured.

"Where's home?"

"At the moment it's London."

"At the moment?" he queried.

"That's one of the answers I came here to find out."

"And have you found your answer?"

"I think I'm starting to see things a bit more clearly."

"I've always believed that you think much more clearly on a full stomach." He grabbed Lani's hand and leapt to his feet, pulling her up with him. "Let's go."

He ushered her along the broad avenue, past the lake and the dinosaur statue, all the while keeping hold of her hand. This time, she didn't snatch it away.

The café bar was located just a few narrow streets behind the Parque Genoves. Tom ordered fried fish and beer for them both.

"Local delicacy," he said.

While they waited for the fish, the waiter brought their drinks and small plates of black olives and locally-cured jamón.

"But of course you need talent as well as luck to be a success..."

It would be easier just to blurt everything out, Lani decided.

"So I live in London with a guy called Charlie, who I met at art college."

"OK," Tom said slowly.

"When we graduated we both moved to London to start a photography company. The plan was for us to become rich and famous. Of course."

"Of course."

"This story is really boring."

"No, I'm fascinated. Truly. Please carry on." He gestured for her to continue.

"We rented a flat, and started the business and, to everyone's amazement, did rather well. We were lucky that a friend from college knew someone that was opening a restaurant. He sent the owner our contact details and he asked us to take some shots. It got us great publicity and loads of new work."

"But you need talent as well as luck to be a success."

"Sure. For the next few months it was great fun, both of us out on shoots, happy because it was working out the way we had planned." Lani paused and took a mouthful of cold beer. "We were working ten hours a day, seven days a week. We were broke and living in a pigsty. We'd forgotten that to run a business invoices have to be sent out, accounts totalled, files filed, photocopying paper ordered and rent to be paid."

"Couldn't you just pay someone?"

Lani snorted. "We were busy but not earning enough money to employ someone. We decided that I would concentrate on the management of the business, and work only part-time out in the field. Charlie would do all the photographic shoots."

"It doesn't sound awfully fair to me."

"I didn't mind. It was only short-term until we had some money in the bank and could afford an assistant."

The waiter arrived with platters of mixed fried fish and a basket of bread. Tom ordered two more beers.

"I've worked night and day for the last eighteen months and I thought that we deserved a break. And with Valentine's Day coming up, I suggested we do a city break, nothing expensive."

"And can I assume Charlie said no?"

"He said that we hadn't quite reached our target yet to justify spending the cash." Lani waved her fork. "This fish is utterly delicious, by the way."

"So, you were upset that he wouldn't go on a break with you?"

"No – not at all. What actually upset me was that I discovered he planned to spend Valentine's Day with a model called Lili. And not ➜

in a professional sense." She looked challengingly at Tom. "I told you it was a boring story."

"I'm sorry."

"I feel such an idiot."

"You're absolutely not. He's a rat."

"Let's drink to that."

"No – let's drink to new friendships instead. Salud."

"Salud," she agreed, and took a gulp of her beer. She raised her glass and clinked his. "And to not allowing rats to ruin my last day in Cadiz."

It was late afternoon when they eventually left the café. Tom looked enquiringly at her.

"Can I ask what you're seeing more clearly now?"

She linked her arm through his.

"I want to be a photographer, and I don't want to live with Charlie."

"That's pretty definite."

"Once I came to the conclusion that I was more upset about being an idiot rather than Charlie being unfaithful, it was quite simple."

She giggled.

"Everything was bouncing about my head so much, I couldn't think straight and I just had to get away. Do you know what I did?"

"No."

"I just grabbed my passport, packed a couple of T-shirts, jumped on the train to Gatwick and booked the first available flight. How impulsive is that?"

"Top marks for crazy."

"As I told you, I just slept, let my brain slow down, and started to think."

"So are you ready for another impulsive moment?"

"What are you talking about?"

He gestured across to his right, to the inviting golden sands of Playa de la Caleta.

"I thought that we should maybe go in for a paddle."

"Now you're crazy. It will be freezing. No, definitely, no…"

Keeping her close, he turned down a set of steps to the beach and walked towards the shore. Lani tried to dig her feet into the sand but he seemed not to notice her puny resistance.

When they reached the water's edge, he stooped to remove his shoes and roll up his trousers.

"This is the Atlantic. Which means that water in front of us was probably an iceberg in the Antarctic yesterday," she protested.

He ignored her.

She sighed, defeated, and bent down to remove her sandals. She crept cautiously towards the sea and let a wave lap gently over her toes.

She hoped someone was finding joy in their happiness

She screamed and retreated onto the warm sand.

"It's freezing."

"Sometimes you just have to go for it." And before she knew what was happening, Tom had wrapped his arm around her waist and sprinted forward into the sea.

Lani burst out laughing, standing knee-deep in the icy-cold water. She wriggled from Tom's grasp and scooping a handful of the water in her palm, lobbed it in his direction. The droplets sparkled as they fell, and Lani recalled the innocent joy of the children splashing in the Plaza de San Juan de Dios fountains. She hoped that somebody was watching them, Tom and her, and finding joy in their happiness.

"Thank you," she whispered, placing a gentle kiss on his cheek. "What happens now, Tom?"

"Isn't it obvious?" he asked, kissing her back. "You have to design an itinerary to beat this when I come to London next week."

She thought of walks through Hyde Park, a boat to Greenwich, the Eye and the two of them drinking mugs of hot chocolate to ward off the cold.

"That won't be a problem."

Friends Forever

One weekend in every year was theirs and theirs alone, no matter what happened

By LIBBY PAGE

Forty years. For forty years June, Helen, Sue and Kathy had gone on holiday together for one weekend every year. It started when they were in their twenties and had just finished their final year of university.

"We need to celebrate," said Kathy, who was the kind of woman who could always find a reason to celebrate and a bottle of something to celebrate it with.

This time they all agreed. After three years of hard work they'd finally done it. They were about to leave the comforts and safety of their college in Durham and to start their real lives.

Not that any of them knew what they wanted to do after graduating, apart from June who had known she was going to be a teacher since she was a child instructing her teddy bears and unfortunate younger sister. She was already signed up to start a teacher training course after the summer, but for the others the future stretched ahead of them like a startlingly blank canvas.

The holiday felt like a perfect way to end their three years of studying and living together.

They went to Paris, with Helen, who had just finished a degree in French, acting as the group's guide and translator. They walked by the Seine in the blazing sunshine, ate pastries in the parks and drank red wine until their lips turned purple.

On their final night they lay under the Eiffel Tower, the ground warm beneath their backs from that day's sun.

"I'm so going to miss living with you all," said Sue after a moment's pause. The other girls said nothing – they couldn't quite find the words

– but instead they reached out for one another's hands, joined together like a concertina of paper dolls.

"We'll stay friends though, won't we?" said June.

"Of course," they all agreed.

"We should do this every year," suggested Kathy, "Whatever we're doing in our lives, wherever we might be, we'll all come together and have one weekend with just us."

And that's how it started. Over the years they have been to Barcelona and Rome, Budapest and Brussels, Florence and the south of France. But also closer to home when budgets or other commitments insisted: a weekend in a Cotswolds cottage, a city break to Edinburgh, a caravan in North Wales.

True to their promise, they have never missed a year.

When Helen moved to Paris, inspired by their weekend together ➤

when she fell in love with the city, they took their trips in France for those years. Eventually she moved back, but not alone – her fiancé Victor came with her. Over the years their husbands – because although Helen was the first, they all eventually found partners and settled down, even Kathy who said she'd be single forever until she met the lovely Malcolm – have come to accept these annual trips away. Sometimes the four husbands meet up when their wives are on holiday, sharing beers and a friendship which is not quite the same as the fierce bond between their wives, but has still grown strong in its own quiet, practical sort of way.

They even kept up their weekends throughout the baby years, altering the "just us" rule slightly to allow for a still breastfeeding child. One year when all four of them had children under four they all found themselves free for one glorious weekend in Cornwall, where the sun shone and they lay on the sand in Harlyn Bay, all too tired to do much else.

"I can't help but feel slightly guilty being here," said June from beneath her large sunhat, "Knowing that Henry is at home on his own with the twins."

Kathy stretched, pushing up her sunglasses. "I don't feel guilty at all. I'm Mum every single other day of the year. Today I'm just me. Sometimes I forget what that feels like."

The other women nodded in understanding.

"And you deserve the break, June," added Sue gently, "Especially after the year you've had."

June's eyes misted, her skin growing suddenly cold despite the sunshine. Her mother had passed away unexpectedly earlier that year. Helen, Sue and Kathy had been there at the funeral with flowers, tissues and strong, loving hugs. Since then June had balanced teaching with looking after her boys and visiting her father several times a week. She hated to admit it, but she felt exhausted.

Helen reached out across the sand for June's hand. "Shall we do a toast to her?" she suggested.

On the Cornwall beach the four women clinked their bottles of beer and lemonade – for Sue who was pregnant again and was planning on telling her friends over dinner that evening.

June cried for her mother but then brushed her eyes, feeling the sun on her face and the warmth of her friends surrounding her.

As time marched on the women found it harder to keep in touch... children grew up, parents aged and the phone calls and visits, which were once a constantly unfurling ribbon, became less frequent. But at least they always had their annual holiday.

When Helen and Victor split up, the women shared frozen margaritas in Madrid that year, and when they got back together they toasted their happiness with prosecco in Venice. New jobs, redundancies, health scares, the trials of raising teenagers... all these and everything else were discussed on these weekends away. Two days where they could focus on one another,

She felt the warmth of her friends surrounding her

where they could reminisce about the years that had passed and think ahead – sometimes nervously, sometimes hopefully – to years the to come.

Which is why Kathy was determined to make the holiday work that year, despite the villa they'd booked in Italy cancelling at the last minute due to a family emergency and her friends' reluctance to organise anything else.

"We'll not find anything at such short notice," said Helen in their WhatsApp group.

"I should probably stay and help with Lara and the little one," wrote June. June's first grandchild, baby Toby, had been born a few months ago. She was the last of her friends to become a grandmother. It broke her heart every time she had to say goodbye to Toby.

"Maybe we should just save the money," said Sue who every year insisted that they all got travel insurance so that were covered for a situation like this. Ever practical and prepared, she was also the one →

to pack insect spray, plasters and pain killers on every holiday.

But Kathy was insistent.

"Forty years!" she reminded them, "It's been forty years and we've never missed a weekend. Not once."

The next day she phoned them all, asking to meet her at her house in Somerset that weekend. Secretly they all felt frustrated. They'd been to Kathy's house countless times, it didn't really count as a holiday. Couldn't they just sit this one out and get on with all the chores that were constantly there waiting for them? But despite their hesitations, they went. After all, it had been forty years.

When they arrived, June collecting the others at the nearby station and, driving them the last part of the journey to Kathy's village, they couldn't quite believe they were in the right place.

"We've never missed a holiday in forty years – not once!"

As they pulled up in the driveway they saw that Kathy's modest garden had been transformed. Bunting and lanterns were hung in the apple tree, colourful blankets carpeted the grass and in the very centre stood a large yurt decorated with multicoloured ribbons. Kathy stood outside the tent, beaming.

"Well?" she said as her friends climbed out of the car, a little slower now than when they were younger, "What do you think?"

The women looked at one another.

"It's beautiful," said Sue.

"But aren't we...?" began June.

"Too old for camping?" finished Helen.

"Nonsense," said Kathy, "Besides, this isn't regular camping."

She showed them into the yurt where four camp beds were lined up, each made up in sheets patterned with superheroes, unicorns and dinosaurs.

"Sorry about the sheets," she said, "I had to improvise and make do with what I have for the grandchildren."

"I shotgun the Superman bed!" shouted June, jumping onto one of the camp beds. The other women burst into laughter.

Throughout the afternoon Malcolm brought the women jugs of cocktails from inside, disappearing quickly again to leave the old friends to catch up.

"I'm afraid I couldn't quite sort portaloos at the last minute," Kathy said, "So you'll have to use the bathroom inside the house."

Nobody minded the break in the illusion.

That night, their voices hoarse from laughing and talking and their cheeks sore from smiling, the women climbed into their camp beds in the yurt.

"What has been your favourite of our holidays?" Sue asked.

"Hmm, I did love Florence," said June, remembering the beautiful buildings and the golden sun.

"I'll always have a soft spot for that first trip to Paris. My life would be so different if we'd never gone," said Helen, "How about you, Sue?"

She thought for a moment. "Remember that time in the caravan in Wales when it rained all weekend?"

The women laughed.

"But that can't really have been your favourite!" exclaimed June.

"But it was," said Sue, "We stayed inside talking for two days."

As the women thought back they suddenly forgot about the rain and remembered those long conversations.

"It's not really about where we go, is it?" added Kathy, "It's actually about being together."

And just like when they were young women lying under the Eiffel Tower, the four friends reached out their hands between the camp beds, holding on to one another. (MW)

A Patchwork Family

Would the sunshine holiday be a bonding experience, or would tempers fray?

By BETH MCKAY

Sarah's heart skipped a beat as the plane touched down. She had always found the moment of landing exciting and it was wonderful to be back in Cyprus. She prodded the seats of the teenagers in front, to remind them to remove their headphones. Reluctantly, they began to stuff their scattered belongings into overflowing backpacks.

George, Sarah's partner, raised a sympathetic eyebrow. The idea of a holiday abroad together had seemed such a tantalising prospect in the gloomy depths of a British winter. Now they were both wondering how a week with two combined families of adolescents would work out in practice.

The first glimpse of the holiday villa lifted Sarah's spirits. The house nestled on a hill below a grove of ancient olive trees, just metres from a pretty, pebbled beach. With its bright, pastel colours, large terrace and lofty, open-plan interior, there was plenty of space for everybody. Even when the inevitable quarrels kicked off about who would have each room, Sarah remained serene. She left George to soothe ruffled feathers and wandered out, barefoot, onto the warm paving stones beside the patio door. It was wonderful to be here in the Mediterranean sunshine, gazing out at a dazzling blue sea.

Peaceful moments became rare, however, as the daily battles over getting up, mealtimes and chores mounted. Sarah's eldest son, Matthew, could be quietly stubborn at the best of times. He rose late every day. He resented being forced to join in jobs or activities with George's twins,

Joel and Ellie. He found it hard enough sharing a room with thirteen-year-old Joel, who talked incessantly from dawn until dusk.

"Mum, get him to stop pestering me!" was Matthew's regular cry of exasperation. Her son was clearly craving some time alone and there seemed to be no chance of that here.

Sarah's middle daughter, Sophie, was kinder to the twins but she still preferred topping up her tan or messaging her friends back home. Tilly, her youngest, moped around. She was anxious to monopolise Sarah's affection and jealous of any time that her mother spent with George. Sarah knew that Tilly still missed her father.

"When will things go back to normal, Mum?" had been her constant question at bedtime, when Sarah first started dating George. After two years, Tilly voiced that hope less often, but she had lost her sense of security.

What was normal these days anyway, Sarah wondered? So many marriages faltered on the road to that fantasy happy ending. Her ex-husband's affair with his female boss was definitely not a prospect that Sarah had entertained when they exchanged rings and vows.

What a relief it had been when George came along, with his honest face and crinkly grin. He had certainly brought her sense of humour ➝

back. More importantly, he had thrown himself wholeheartedly into the rich tapestry of their complicated new life. With five children between them, it really was a juggling act. The unfamiliar role of being a step-parent was full of more pitfalls than either Sarah or George could ever have imagined. One of other of them was always getting things wrong.

In the end, it was the swimming pool that rescued the holiday dream. Matthew was sitting on the edge, dangling long, pale legs in the water, listening to his favourite band on his new Beats headphones. Sophie was sprawled beside him on a towel, her face concealed beneath a floppy hat and shades.

It was Tilly of all people who started the water fight, with Joel and Ellie. Soon the three younger children were shrieking and jumping in and out of the pool with excitement.

Matthew was oblivious until a large, wet ball hit him on the side of the head. Joel froze, waiting nervously for his reaction. It was an accident of course. He had been aiming for Tilly, who was grinning with mischief from behind her big brother's shoulders.

"Hey!" Matthew shouted. His face flushed with fury. He stared hard at his young adversary.

Tilly tickled her brother in the ribs before he could explode and whipped away Matthew's headphones.

"It was me, silly! Joel wasn't aiming at you!" She danced off with the Beats and threw them on a sun lounger. She just made it back into the pool in time, dripping water all over Sophie as she dived past her. Suddenly all five of them were in the pool, splashing and laughing.

Sarah put her arm round George when he came in to fetch the ice lollies.

"They'll need these," he beamed. "It's good to see them all playing."

"They look like a proper family," Sarah replied happily. She watched Matthew drape a brotherly arm around Joel's shoulder as the pair tried to pour a jug of water over Tilly's head.

Tilly's smile, as she escaped their clutches, was brighter than the sun above their heads. ⓜⓌ

Lost Luggage

People loaned him bright pink shorts and baggy swimming trunks… could Eric cope?

By CAMILLA KELLY

ILLUSTRATION: ISTOCKPHOTO

"Why does this sort of thing always happen to you?" Annie said, trying not to smile. She knew Eric well enough now to doubt that he'd have a sense of humour over this. He was a sensitive soul.

Sure enough, Eric's was the only unhappy face in the whole of the resort bar. Around them, the rest of the newly arrived tourists were enjoying the Portugal sun and the deliciousness of the first drink of their holidays, and everyone was beginning to unwind.

Everyone except Eric.

"I don't know!" he cried, his head in his hands.

"Cheer up. The airline promised your bags will be here in a day or two," she said. "And all you need until then is a pair of shorts."

She almost said, "Aren't you glad I talked you into a beach holiday rather than that walking tour of Prague you liked the look of?" but thought it might be pushing things a bit.

She and Eric had been seeing each other for nearly six months now and while she was very fond of him, lately she'd been wondering if her feelings really were strong enough to overcome the differences between them.

Eric was kind-hearted and full of integrity. From day one, when he'd gotten his work suit all muddy while helping her fix the chain that had come off her bicycle outside the insurance office where he worked, she'd felt him to be exactly the kind of man she could consider building a life with. He'd even found her a plaster from the office first aid kit for her skinned knee, and pampered her with hot sweet tea while she recovered from the very slight tumble she'd taken.

"I'm trying to take your mind off your clothes," she said, kissing him

She'd been delighted when he accepted her invitation to come and see a pantomime at the small theatre she worked for.

After that they were together all the time. She thought the world of him. She just wished he wasn't so... serious all the time.

For their first holiday together they'd picked a cheap and cheerful package trip – somewhere sunny and fun where they could just relax and enjoy each other's company.

Then this had to happen.

They were joined at the bar by a couple from their tour group whom they'd met at the airport. Johnny and Shirley were in their fifties, and joined at the hip. Johnny's voice was as loud as his bright Hawaiian shirt; Shirley was carrying an equally bright cocktail.

"Alright, old man?" Johnny said to Eric. "Did you have any luck with the baggage handlers?"

"Apparently his bag has been sent to Dubai," Annie said.

She could tell Eric was trying not to mind being called "old man" by someone maybe thirty years older than him. She felt the urge to smile again so bit her lip.

"I'll have to go shopping and buy a few things," Eric said.

"No need for that!" Shirley said. "Johnny will have a few things to keep you going. Won't you, love?"

Annie snorted into her drink. She was ashamed of how much the idea delighted her. Eric threw her a panicked look. She just knew that this would confirm every suspicion he had about the universe conspiring against him.

Johnny offered to drop something off at Eric's room that he could wear, and since Eric seemed utterly speechless, Annie thanked Johnny on his behalf.

He was just being kind," she said the next morning, when Eric stood in front of her wearing the shorts and T-shirt that Johnny had loaned him – as well as an Eyore-ish expression, all world weary.

"I'll just wear the same trousers as yesterday…" he said.

"Don't do that – you'll bake. Besides, Johnny might be offended."

"But look at me!" Eric cried.

They were the boldest pink shorts Annie had ever seen.

"I think you look cool," she said. "Very metrosexual… a bit David Beckham, even." On impulse she leaned forward and kissed him.

"What was that for?" he said, reddening slightly.

"I was trying to take your mind off your clothes and remind you that we're here on our first holiday together. It's very romantic, you know."

He smiled and slipped an arm around her. When the worry lines left his forehead he looked like a completely different person – young and handsome. She kissed him again. For a while he seemed to forget about his lost luggage.

Later, a stranger stopped Eric at the breakfast buffet. "Hey mate, bad luck about your luggage. I've a spare pair of swimming trunks you can borrow if you like?" ➡

"Who was that?" Eric whispered to Annie after the man moved off.

"Not sure... No, wait a minute – I think I was chatting to his girlfriend yesterday... oh, and look – they're sitting with Johnny and Shirley. Let's go and join them."

Eric was reluctant.

"He's just being friendly," Annie said. "And you do need trunks."

"Can you imagine if I borrowed his? He'd make two of me!"

"But don't you want to get in the pool today?" It was scorching hot. "And," she said cajolingly, "it's only until your suitcase turns up. Take the kindness."

He sighed. "Oh, alright."

Johnny wolf-whistled as Eric and Annie approached his table.

"Blimey, Eric, where'd you get those sexy shorts? I honestly didn't know you had it in you!"

Eric's face reddened but everyone was so good-humoured he was soon laughing along with them. There was only so long you could feel self-conscious, Annie supposed, as she saw him start to relax. In fact, after a while, she looked at him sitting in the bright pink shorts and fluorescent T-shirt, and thought she hadn't seen him so animated in a long time.

The swimming trunks were another revelation – they were so big for Eric he had to wear a belt with them!

He came cautiously to the pool as if trying to make himself invisible, obviously hoping no one would notice him, but as soon as the owner of the trunks saw him, he bellowed, "Eric!"

It felt – even to Annie, standing beside Eric – that the entire population of the hotel turned to look.

She came closer to Eric, suddenly feeling very protective. Eric waved bashfully at their snickering audience. Then he hoiked up his shorts with an exaggerated movement, and did a pratfall into the water!

When he came up everyone was laughing. He looked for Annie and gave her a helpless shrug, and a smile.

Everyone thought his situation was so funny that word soon spread.

At first Annie was afraid the teasing might bother him, but he took it all so good-naturedly she was proud of him. The fame even seemed to bring him out of his shell. He didn't have to worry about introducing himself or be the shy wallflower since everyone knew who he was.

As each day passed and his luggage failed again to turn up, more and more people volunteered bits of clothing. By the end of the week there was hardly anyone in their group who hadn't loaned him something to wear.

At one time his Metallica T-shirt got them a free taxi ride. At another his Harry Potter shirt got him an extra scoop of ice cream.

"This is ridiculous," he said to Annie. "I can't keep taking people's charity like this. I should go and buy some things."

He didn't have to be a wallflower since everyone knew who he was

"Can't you see how much everyone is enjoying this? Shirley told me yesterday she doesn't even let Johnny wear that shirt you wore to the Old Town."

"So everyone's enjoying me making an idiot out of myself?" But he added a soft smile.

"You're not an idiot." She came close to him and pulled his arms around her. "You're having fun, you're a good sport, and you're making a dozen new friends… and you're impressing me more and more every minute."

The holiday was bringing out the best in him. He was the kind of person who'd be careful not to offend anyone who offered him help, and was sensitive to everyone's feelings and always showed gratitude. Seeing the way he responded to the silliness of the outfits he'd been given and how charming and self-effacing he was, Annie was reminded of all the things she'd found attractive about him in the first place.

When one night they were having dinner at a beautiful old restaurant, and two girls from their hotel spotted them and invited themselves to join them, Annie was almost annoyed. Eric →

cast her a quick glance that said, *What can you do?* and they spent the rest of the evening laughing and trying every kind of dessert on the menu. It was fun, but not exactly the romantic night Annie had been hoping for.

On their last night a dinner and dance was held at the resort. Their rep felt so bad about not being able to get Eric's luggage back that he offered to lend Eric something of his own to wear.

Annie had been looking forward to the evening. She had a new dress, it was a beautiful starry night, and she was going to do her best to make it a very memorable time with Eric.

They were set to meet in the lobby of the hotel. She was curious to see what he would be wearing this evening and hoped it was something reasonably suitable. Their rep was a fairly smart dresser, however he was a good deal shorter than Eric.

Everyone who had loaned Eric clothes throughout the week was there

Eric was waiting for her when she came down and she almost didn't recognise him. He was dressed in a sharply cut suit, a crisp grey shirt, and he even had a red flower in his lapel.

Annie paused to stare at him. He looked wonderful.

"That's one of our rep's suits?" she asked him.

"No, actually, this is one of my suits. My suitcase finally arrived about half an hour ago."

"Perfect timing," she said with a smile.

After a week of seeing a different Eric every time he changed clothes, it was something of a relief to see him back to being himself. As much as she'd enjoyed the game of it, she realised she'd missed the original Eric too. There was so much to love in him.

"Ready to go?" he said, galantly offering her his arm.

When they walked into dinner together a cheer rose up and Eric took a modest bow.

Annie had to do a double take.

Everyone who had loaned Eric clothes throughout the week was there – and each and every one of them was wearing clothes variously too long, too small, too short, or just plain inappropriate.

"Eric! Are those your clothes?" she exclaimed.

Even Shirley was wearing a polo shirt and flip flops.

Eric laughed.

"We thought it was only fair that I return the favour to everyone."

Annie giggled too. It was far from the formal evening she'd expected, but this would be much more fun – and she drew out her camera to record the event.

"I've had a fantastic holiday," Eric said suddenly. "I just wanted you to know that."

"Oh, me too," Annie said.

She felt sorry she'd ever doubted him. She knew for certain now that she wanted a future with him – and hoped that he felt the same.

"You've put up with so much. I don't know how you've been able to do it," she said.

He pulled her close for a kiss. "It's because it would be impossible ever to feel anything but proud, standing next to you," he said. 🆆

The Open Road

The little yellow camper van up for sale was a green light for Rosie's dreams…

By ROSANNA LEY

Rosie had always loved travelling. They'd planned to do more of it once David retired. But sadly, his diagnosis put an end to that particular dream. Rosie liked to be around for her daughter Melissa, son-in-law Jake and her three grandchildren – even more, since losing David.

Still. When she saw the ad in the local paper, something tugged at her heartstrings – a half-forgotten sense of excitement from long ago.

At first, she put it out of her mind. She had a busy life. She still missed David, but she filled her days by volunteering at the local charity shop, looking after the grandchildren and learning French.

"French?" Melissa had raised an eyebrow when she first told her. "Don't take this the wrong way – but isn't it a bit late to be learning a new language, Mum?"

"It exercises the brain," Rosie said.

But it wasn't just that, was it? Even then, she'd been nurturing the dream.

Later that day, she read the ad again. Why not? No harm in looking, she thought. It would probably have gone by now, but…

She rang the number. A young woman answered. She sounded harassed. "Yes, it's still available," she said. "Come round."

So Rosie did.

The little camper van was sunshine yellow and very cute.

"Take a look." The young woman unlocked it. "Me and Carl used to go everywhere in this little beauty, but…" She glanced with rueful affection at the two young children playing in the garden.

"I understand." It had been like that for Rosie and David too. Once the kids were born, they'd put so many plans aside. David had preferred to

travel in comfort and style, whereas Rosie had always been more of an adventurer. And she'd always longed for a camper van...

Inside, it was perfect. There was a little cooker, a fridge, a fold-down bed – everything you could possibly want.

"You and your husband going off travelling then?" the young woman asked her.

"No husband," Rosie told her. "He died two years ago. It's just me."

She waved away the woman's apology. She wasn't to know. And what sane woman of sixty-two bought a camper van to go away in alone?

"I'll take it," she heard herself say.

"You've done what?" Melissa stared at her.

"I've bought a camper van," Rosie repeated.

"But..." For once, her daughter was lost for words.

"Good for you," said Jake. "When's the maiden voyage?"

Rosie smiled. "Mid-June," she said. "If you can manage without me."

"Of course we can." Jake nodded approvingly.

"But where are you going, Mum?"

"To France." It seemed the obvious choice. She thought of the pretty villages, the pine forests, the ocean. France welcomed camper vans, and... she could put those French lessons to use at last.

"France?" She may as well have said Timbuktu.

Rosie hated seeing the anxiety in her daughter's eyes. Since losing ➔

her father, Melissa had clung on to what she had left. She just wanted her mother to be safe, not gallivanting to France in a camper van.

"I'll only stay in official camping spots," Rosie reassured her. "And I'll have breakdown insurance."

She was nervous, of course. She'd never driven a camper van and she hadn't been away on her own for years. But alongside the nerves, excitement was beating like the rhythm of a distant drum. The open road was calling her. Rosie hadn't lost that yearning for adventure. And if she didn't do it now, when would she?

She took the camper over on the ferry from Portsmouth and drove at a leisurely pace to the West Coast. Melissa had promised to text her every day. But Rosie found that there were plenty of other camper-vanners to talk to – everyone was very helpful and friendly. And much as Rosie loved her home and her family, it was exciting – exploring a different landscape, meeting new people, feeling at one with nature as she trundled along in her sunshine-yellow camper.

At the coast, she parked next to another camper van. A man in his mid-sixties was sitting outside and they smiled and said hello.

Later, as Rosie was putting the kettle on, she heard a voice.

"Hi."

It was her neighbour. He had a cheerful smile and warm blue eyes.

"Sorry to disturb you." He waggled the empty milk carton he was holding. "I wondered if you could spare a drop of milk?"

"Of course."

Rosie ended up making him a cup of tea and they sat outside watching the sun go down and chatting. His name was Geoff, he liked walking and cycling, and he lived in Hampshire, not far from Rosie in West Sussex. He'd spent most of his life working in an office, he told her, grimacing. Now he was retired, he wanted to make the most of being outdoors.

"It's now or never," Rosie murmured. After all, none of them were getting any younger.

"Exactly," he said.

When they realised how long they'd spent chatting, he returned to his van and Rosie made supper which she ate outside looking at the stars.

Later, she messaged Melissa.

Are you all right, Mum? Are you lonely?

I'm fine, Rosie messaged back. *And no, I'm not lonely. Not at all.*

The following morning, Geoff's camper van had already disappeared by the time Rosie set off for her new destination.

As she drove into the next campsite, Rosie saw a camper van she recognised. She felt a small lurch of pleasure. How funny. Should she park next to him again or would he think she was stalking him? She laughed. What did she have to lose?

> *She swam in the cool Atlantic, diving into the waves like a girl*

Rosie spent the rest of the day exploring. She went for a walk along the sandy pathways of the pine forest, relishing the scent of the pine resin mixed with ozone and wild thyme, until she reached a dusty boardwalk leading to the ocean. She stripped down to her swimsuit and swam in the cool Atlantic, gasping as the waves caught her, diving into them as if she was a young girl again.

Breathless and exhilarated, she came ashore. What would Melissa say if she could see her now?

Back at the campsite, Geoff was manning a barbecue. Delicious smells wafted into the air and Rosie realised how hungry she was.

"Hey Rosie," he called. "Great to see you. Can I tempt you to supper?"

He certainly could. Rosie contributed a bottle of local French wine she'd bought in the village and they feasted on fresh fish, charred red peppers and vine tomatoes, the juices mopped up with crusty French bread. Heaven, thought Rosie.

They talked non-stop – about their lives, their work, their families. Like Rosie, Geoff was close to his two daughters and grandchildren. Like Rosie, he had lost his spouse – but in Geoff's case, sadly, to another man many years ago.

→

"It's better this way." He sipped his wine. "Jen and I had very different interests. We just drifted apart."

Rosie squeezed his arm in sympathy.

"And you never met anyone else?"

She knew she'd been lucky with David. Like all couples they'd had ups and downs, but they'd always been strong enough to get through.

"Nope." Geoff shrugged. "Maybe living on my own made me selfish."

They both laughed. Rosie knew what he meant – but she didn't think it was true. He was a kind man and very good company.

Once again, time had flown and Rosie had to force herself up and away back to her van, which suddenly seemed just a little cold and lonely.

"You might think this is a stupid idea…" Geoff said uncertainly

In the morning, Geoff came round for coffee and they pored over the maps together, discussing where they were heading next. It turned out they had the same plan – to travel down the West Coast as far as Biarritz and then if time permitted, spend a few days in the Pyrenees.

"You might think this is a stupid idea," Geoff said. "But why don't we do the rest of our trip together? Meet up at the campsites, have dinner sometimes, maybe the odd trip out?" He sounded uncertain, as if unsure of her reaction.

"It's a great idea." Rosie was delighted. She hadn't been looking for a travelling companion, but now that she'd found one… This adventure was getting better by the day.

And so, they spent the remainder of Rosie's holiday travelling in tandem. They walked in pine forests, swam in the wild ocean and went to restaurants when Geoff wasn't cooking up a storm on the barbie.

But all too soon it was their final day. Rosie was off home and Geoff was heading to Southern France for another week before he too returned.

Rosie felt rather sad during their last night out at a local restaurant. She'd had such a good time. She already felt close to him, this fellow-traveller who had become a friend. She was looking forward to seeing the family, but she couldn't help thinking that it would be hard to settle back into her old life – without travelling, without outdoors living, and yes, without Geoff.

She wasn't sure that it meant so much to Geoff though. When they said goodnight, he made no move to kiss her, even though she'd been so hoping that he would.

Now or never, she thought. So, she stood on tiptoe, put her hands on his broad shoulders and kissed him. He looked a bit surprised and then to her delight, he kissed her back.

"Good night, Geoff."

Had she been wrong to cross the line? After all, they were no spring chickens and Geoff had never given her any sign that he wanted to be more than friends.

In the morning, Rosie set off in the van before Geoff was up and about. It had been a marvellous adventure, she told herself. But she had to accept that now, it was over.

Back home, Melissa and Jake wanted all the details and she told them everything – everything that was, except the kiss.

"And will you be going travelling again, Mum?" Melissa asked.

"Oh, I hope so." Rosie glanced wistfully outside to where her sunshine-yellow camper van was parked in the drive.

"You should do," her daughter surprised her by saying. "It's done you good. You're looking great."

Later that evening, Rosie's phone rang. It was Geoff.

"I was wondering…" Once again he sounded unsure.

"Yes?"

"If maybe we could meet up when I get back to the UK? Make plans for another trip." He hesitated. "Would you be up for that, Rosie?"

"Oh yes," she said. "I certainly would."

Perhaps Geoff was just shy. Perhaps he, too, was looking for adventure. And she felt it again – that small lurch of excitement. It lay ahead of her full of possibilities… The invitation of the open road. (MW)

Singles Holiday

Sam absolutely can go on holiday, all on her own... and so that's what she does

By LYNDA FRANKLIN

I am boyfriendless, and to all intents and purposes, girlfriendless. By that, I mean that all my present female friends are in relationships, and that appears to leave very little time for me at the moment.

Hence my decision to holiday alone this year.

"Are you sure you really want to do that?" My friend Lou has been dating for three months now. "Isn't that just for people who have no friends?"

"Or for people who want to get away from their friends, maybe – you never know."

I smile at her confidently, as if I really want to holiday on my own.

"I always think people who holiday on their own are a bit odd. I'd take a few books to read round the pool. It would be really embarrassing to look – well – on your own."

"I will be on my own, Lou."

"Well, yes, I know – even so –" She peters out, looking a bit awkward. "Still, I bet you have a really great time. In fact I quite envy you!"

I tell Lisa next, my loyal forever childhood friend. We laugh at the same ridiculous things, and share the same taste in wine and food.

We share everything – more or less – except for our taste in men. Lisa has been in a relationship with Damion for over a year now, and every time I meet him, he irritates me more.

"Come with us, Sam," she urges, giving me a look that shows she feels sorry for me. "We're going glamping in the Lake District, and I know Damion won't mind. He likes you. You can't go on holiday on your own!"

"Of course I can. Loads of people do."

I want to add that anything is better than glamping with Damion, but fight the urge.

"But what on earth will you do? Who will you speak to?"

"For goodness' sake, Lisa, I'm not going to be the only person on the plane, or in the hotel, and certainly not on the beach. Perhaps I didn't explain, but I've decided against going to the moon after all."

Lisa laughs. "Oh you know what I mean. I just can't think of anything worse than holidaying alone."

"Can't you?" I push thoughts of Damion away and redouble my efforts to look positive. "Well, I'm looking forward to it. I can go anywhere I want, and don't have to please anyone."

"Yes – but on your own?"

I nod. "Lou said that she envied me."

➡

"Well, if you believe that –" Lisa stops when she sees my face. "Look, why don't you go away with your family this year? I bet they'd love to have you with them."

"Squashed in Dad's old motorhome with Mum and my sister Molly?"

"Well it has to be better than being on your own, surely?"

"Nope. Don't think so."

She gives up after that, and tells me maybe I shouldn't have given Ryan his marching orders so quickly.

"I'm not prepared to put up with someone who doesn't notice my hair's a shade darker, or I'm wearing a new dress…"

Even as I'm saying it, I realise I must have been in a really awful mood that day. I mean it's important to notice these things, but it also seems a little on the trivial side now.

Anyway, Ryan and his total lack of awareness are history now.

For goodness sake come with us." Mum says over dinner. "It'll be lovely, just like the old days. All of us together in the motorhome again. We've got a barbecue now, you know."

"That's nice."

"That's what I'm trying to tell you, Sam – we've got all mod cons."

"Mod cons? What on earth are they?"

"Mum means we can eat burgers instead of sandwiches." My sister grins. Molly is fifteen, and already planning a holiday with her friends next year. "We've got new sleeping bags, too, haven't we, Mum?"

I know she is winding Mum up, but Mum nods cheerily.

"Yes, I got them in the New Year sale. They're lovely, Sam. Really warm."

"I suppose you'll need that where you're going." I try to look smug. "I'm going to be somewhere hot and sunny myself. So, you see, I won't be needing a sleeping bag."

"I suppose I could always come with you." Molly says hopefully.

"You're not old enough yet, Molly," Mum says in a voice probably more suited to addressing a five-year-old.

"In another year or so, perhaps."

Molly shrugs and I smile at her. When she's older, it will be rather nice to go on holiday with my sister. Perhaps we'll both be alone and friendless by then, drifting into old age and companionship together. People will say, *You know Sam and Molly – that pair of sisters who live together in that old derelict house. No one ever visits them. They haven't got a friend in the world –*

"Pudding?"

"What?" I snap back to reality. I really need to book this holiday, and book it quickly. A week in the sun catching up with all my chick-lit books will be brilliant. Wine on tap, snacks on the side. I'm actually rather warming to it.

So here I am – sundrenched Lake Garda – stretched out on a sunbed by the pool, drink in one hand, book in the other. I've brought lots with me, but am re-reading *Bridget Jones.* I find I have a great deal of empathy with her at the moment.

It's all so beautiful. I wish I had someone to share it with

And who knows, somewhere out there in the heat of the Italian sun could be my own Mr Darcy. So far I've only managed to meet two girls who giggle a lot.

I take a sip of cold orangeade, telling myself firmly how wonderful it is to be free.

This evening there's to be one of those awful getting-to-know-you events. Free drink and buffet are to be provided, and I have a horrible feeling that the giggle girls will make a beeline for me. I decide to take myself off for a walk along the beach instead.

I take my time meandering across the sand, dipping my toes in the warm water, and gazing at the stunning sunset that's turning the sky brilliant orange. It's all so beautiful, and suddenly I wish I had someone to share it with. Suddenly I don't want to be here on my own.

I send off a couple of quick texts to Lou and Lisa but get no reply. →

They are probably out and having a brilliant time with their boyfriends.

I even consider texting Molly, but decide against it. I think even hearing about drizzly London might make me homesick at the moment.

Suddenly my head reels and I stumble backwards into the soft sand. I lie there for a second, trying to make sense of what just happened.

"Oh blimey – look, I'm so sorry – are you all right?"

Turning my head slightly to the left, I see the large red ball an inch from my nose that practically knocked me out. I stay still for a few minutes, then take the proffered hand to help me up.

"I'm sorry. We were just having a kick around – are you OK?"

Typical. I can't even manage to get myself knocked to the ground by a hunky dreamy-eyed Italian. He sounds as English as me, and judging by the look of the ball, about fifteen.

"I'm OK – I think," I say, flicking sand from my face. "Pity you didn't manage to see me in this big, deserted beach –"

He's looking down at me, all six foot of him, and he's definitely not fifteen. A few feet away a couple of his friends are looking on. Waiting to see if I'm still alive, I suppose.

"Really sorry," he says again, and I notice he's tanned, wearing blue shorts and no top, and has a rather nice smile. "Sure you're all right?"

"I'm fine, really."

He laughs, breathes a loud sigh of relief, and holds out his hand. "I'm James, by the way – James Darcy."

"Oh –" Suddenly I come over all Bridget Jones. This has to be fate. "I'm Sam."

I'm so glad I'm wearing my white cotton dress and have not yet turned bright red in the sun.

"Fancy a drink at the beach bar? The least I can do is buy you refreshments after sending you flying."

I smile back at him, deciding a headache is worth this encounter. "Thanks. I'd like that."

The sun is low in the sky now, the sand still hot under our feet, and as we wander off towards the bar, I have the distinct feeling this holiday is going to turn out OK after all. 🆆

Cornish Adventures

Always the same, yet never the same – that's the beauty of the sea

By GILLIAN HARVEY

Sally closed her eyes and breathed in. The stinging, salt air hit the back of her throat like a slap. It was always cold, the air; even when summer was on its breath. The sea chilled it and sent it racing across the front bringing its own particular brand of freshness.

That's why people went on holiday abroad, she supposed. The heat. She'd liked it too – twenty-five years ago in her bikini with her headphones and a book. Now she found it oppressive; preferred to ➤

spend time exploring, walking – even swimming when she felt brave enough.

The kids had used to complain – there was nothing to do in Cornwall, at the little old farmhouse where they habitually stayed. Now, in their early 20s, they still came along occasionally, grateful for the break from the pace of their new lives as adults – even grateful, sometimes, for the patchy signal. A proper, immersive detachment from the pull of their mobile phones.

This time, it was just her and Bill, making the journey of six and a half hours – two stops, one picnic and a breather when they first hit the seafront. They'd got it down to a tee. Fish and chips, sitting on the windswept pavilion overlooking Polzeath, meandering back along the narrow, sea-view roads and into the cottage in time to get the kettle on and watch the news.

"Do you think we're set in our ways?" she'd asked this time when they were rinsing the teacups.

"Never," he'd smiled. "Or at least, not in the ways that matter."

This morning, she'd woken early and taken the two-mile walk down to the front on her own. The air was always cool in the morning, often misty – you could be forgiven sometimes for thinking that it was the middle of winter. Then around ten, the sunlight would finally penetrate even the worst of it and you could be on the beach in a bikini and having to slap on sun-cream.

The sea in Cornwall was changeable, too. Its waves at times crashing, mighty towers of water that took out even the hardiest surfer. Then calm, stretching for miles to the horizon. They could change at a moment's notice. Yet somehow the sea remained timeless.

"Don't you get tired of going to the same place every year?" Georgie, one of her closest friends, had asked her once.

"No," she'd said. "Because it is never the same."

She thought back to the first time she'd stood at this spot, her belly swelling gently beneath her summer dress. "It's beautiful," she'd whispered to Bill. They were newly married; his parents had booked the cottage for them as a treat. She'd scoffed at the idea of it. To her, holidays had meant passports and planes and sunshine.

"Go and relax," his mum had said. "It'll be good for all three of you."

They'd laughed when they'd turned up at the tumbledown cottage with its worse-for-wear kitchen and tangled garden. "Not that relaxing," Bill had laughed as they'd struggled to open the front door.

But once they'd settled in and enjoyed the cream tea the owner had left as a welcome gift, they'd begun to see its charm. The following year they'd returned – Grace just three months old.

Now the house was steeped in memories and even though it belonged to someone else, they felt that it was theirs – their holiday home. It was comforting, sitting in the evening, recounting things they had done in years gone by – and talking too about the things to come.

She'd been shaken earlier this year when Grace had rung to tell her she was pregnant. Delighted, of course, but shaken too. 'Grandmother' – she tested the word on her tongue and it seemed to have nothing to do with her. Grandmothers were old, weren't they?

Now she imagined holding the baby in her arms; loving him. How she and Bill had embraced each change in their lives together – and how, essentially, she'd be fifty-five years old this year whether she was a grandmother or not.

She thought about the beach – how it was constantly changing. How there were dangers and rainclouds and enormous waves; but these would yield to sunshine and blue skies and calm seas. How, despite it all, every aspect had its own beauty. And the storms only made the moments of calm more precious.

She watched the clouds scuttle across the sky and felt the temperature dip. Tiny drops of rain began to hit her bare shoulders quite pleasantly before becoming heavier.

By the time she arrived back at the cottage, she was drenched. Then, of course, the sun came out brilliant and strong, making it look as if she'd taken a dip in a ditch.

"What happened to you?" Bill asked, as she walked into the kitchen.

"Oh, nothing." She smiled. "Just another adventure." 🆆

123

It's All Greek To Me

She was meant to be recapturing her youth on Corfu, but Bev's heart ached

By ISABELLE BROOM

B everly reached across to pick up her piña colada and swirled her finger around in the glass. She had left it sitting there for so long that the pineapple juice had separated from the coconut cream, though this did little to deter her from drinking it.

"Waste not, want not" was one of Beverly's most-repeated phrases. She had said it so often to the children when they were growing up that it had become habit, and since they'd both moved away from home, she'd started rolling it out to her husband Frank instead.

The two of them had bickered about it only the previous week, when he'd accused her of being a "feeder" because she'd insisted he finish up the last of the apple pie.

"Careful, Bev," came a voice from the sun lounger beside her own. "The wind might change, and you'll be stuck forever with that scowl on your face."

Beverly gave her best friend a sidelong glance. Lara always had been able to read her emotions as if they were words scribbled across her forehead.

"I was just thinking about Frank," she admitted. "About how he didn't so much as bat a bloomin' eyelid when I announced that we were flying out here, as if me not being at home for my fiftieth was of absolutely no concern to him."

Lara had begun reapplying sun lotion to her legs, her teeth set in concentration as she attempted to reach the back of her thighs.

"I wouldn't worry about it," she said blithely. "You know what men are like.'

"That's just it, though," Beverly said, frowning as she watched her friend twist around like a circus contortionist. "We allow men to get away with so much unacceptable behaviour because we indulge their thoughtlessness rather than pulling them up on it."

Lara was pink-cheeked now from exertion, her bikini bottoms askew from all the wriggling around.

"Don't you think you're overreacting a bit?" she replied. "Frank knows how much you love Corfu – perhaps he was just pleased that you were going to spend your birthday here."

Her friend was half right. Beverly did love Corfu – especially the tiny resort of Kalami, with its sprawling cactus plants, crystal clear sea and abundant local cat population. It was also the setting for the famous White House, once lived in by Lawrence Durrell and now a holiday home with a stunning waterfront restaurant attached.

Beverly looked up at it now, imagining as she always did the figure of Lawrence at an upstairs window, his gaze on the splendid view of the bay as he conjured up characters for his next book. All of Greece was steeped in myth and history, but as far as Beverly was ➜

concerned, Corfu was the country's most precious gem. She was glad Lara had invited her.

"What better way to celebrate turning fifty than by coming away with me and behaving exactly like we did in our twenties?" she had enthused. And Beverly, despite having no desire to recapture the bumpy years she had willingly traded to begin a family with the man she loved, had found herself agreeing to the plan.

She'd assumed that Frank and the kids – she must stop calling them "the kids" – would never stand idly by and let her vanish abroad when such an important, milestone birthday was looming.

But they had. And so, here she was.

"He didn't even seem sorry to see me go," Beverly continued bitterly, draining the last of her cocktail with a slurp. "I modelled my holiday wardrobe for him to get his attention, but when I asked him which dress suited me best, he shrugged and said it was all Greek to him. His idea of a joke I expect."

Lara squinted across at her, raising a hand to shield her eyes. It was nearing six now, and the sun was beginning its honey-drizzle descent towards the horizon. The faint breeze that lifted the hairs on Beverly's arms was gentle as a whisper, and she could detect a faint tang of lemons in the air.

The staff at the beachside restaurants would begin their nightly ritual of stacking up loungers and setting tables soon, but Beverly was not ready to leave yet. Now that the dazzling heat of the day was beginning to soften, she felt as if she could luxuriate in its more comforting warmth.

Or she could have, if she wasn't feeling quite so sad.

Do you remember the first time we ever came here?" Lara said, laughing as Beverly rolled her eyes. "Don't make that face! You know as well as I do that those were the best two weeks of our lives up to that point, before we had to worry about husbands and babies and which night to put the bins out. Back then, it felt as if anything was possible."

Beverly nodded, smiling at the image of herself as a twenty-one-year-old. She had been feisty, fearless and full of boundless energy – they both had.

She felt sorry for young people today, burdened as they were by the pressures of social media, earning a pittance in their post-graduate jobs despite being saddled with a vast debt and extortionate rents. How any of them were expected to save the requisite thousands of pounds towards a house deposit, Beverly had no idea.

It was why she and Frank had made sure to put something by for Mark and Deborah. As soon as they were ready to buy a property, there would be a lump sum waiting.

"Would you go back to those days, if you could?" Lara asked. "If a Greek genie popped up from underneath that jetty over there and offered you a wish for your birthday, would you whisk us back to 1971?"

> "If he married and had children he's probably a wreck like us"

"No!" Beverly spluttered. "Back to being broke, arguing with my mum – and doing everything I could to make Kostas the waiter notice me? No thanks."

"Kostas!" cried Lara. "God, he was dreamy. Neither of us had ever seen such a chiselled, tanned and manly man before. What was it he used to call us?"

"Koukla," said Beverly. "It means doll."

"That's right!" Lara sniggered. "He made us feel so special, when in reality, he probably said the same thing to all the girls."

"No probably about it," drawled Beverly.

"Do you think he's still on the island?" said Lara. "I'd love to see him again, see how the years have treated him."

"If he got married and had children, he's probably a wreck like us."

Beverly chuckled as her friend's expression turned indignant.

"I'll have you know," she said primly, "that fifty is the new thirty – or so I read. You and I, Bev, are in the prime of our lives."

"Sure," Beverly deadpanned. "And when we're in our eighties, ➔

someone will write an article about how octogenarianism is the new adolescence."

"What do you think Frank will be like in his eighties?" prompted Lara, making kissy noises as a kitten scampered into view. Her friend had insisted on a trip to Kalami's supermarket the moment they arrived, purely to stock up on treats for Corfu's army of felines.

Beverly pictured her husband, with his broad shoulders, salt-and-pepper beard and easy smile, feeling absurdly as if she might cry.

"I think he'll be a liability," she said stonily. "Just like he is now."

Lara had scooped the kitten up into her arms. Beverly could hear its contented purr over the tender sigh and swish of the sea.

> "I could come home with a neck tattoo and he wouldn't murmur"

"He's really upset you, hasn't he?" said Lara, and again, Beverly was forced to blink back treacherous tears.

"He's just been so evasive lately," she said. "He keeps going out into the back garden to make phone calls, and the other night I heard him clanking around under the stairs. What if he's hiding something from me, Lara? What if he's having an—"

She could not quite bring herself to say the word "affair".

"No," soothed Lara. "There's about as much chance of Kostas the waiter still being sexy as there is of Frank doing the dirty on you. The man's besotted."

"He's not," wailed Beverly. "He barely notices me. I could come home from this holiday with a neck tattoo and dreadlocks, and he wouldn't so much as murmur. I'm basically invisible. I mean, I must be, otherwise he'd at least have got me something for my birthday, he'd at least have cared that he was going to miss it."

She was aware she had begun to rant, but Lara did not seem perturbed. She kept glancing past Beverly along the beach, seemingly finding the view far more interesting than her friend's neuroses. Perhaps this was what life was like after fifty – maybe she was destined to be overlooked by everyone in her life whom she cared about?

"I might just go back up to the apartment for a bit," she said.

"No!" Lara winced as the startled kitten leapt from her lap, its tiny claws leaving welts on her bare thighs. "Let's at least have another drink," she urged.

Beverly sighed. She may as well blot out her feelings with alcohol.

"And as it's your birthday," said Lara, "how about we go to The White House?"

They took the beach route, picking their careful way over the jagged rocks along the shoreline before taking a set of rough stone steps up the hill. Beverly stalled as they drew closer to the front of the house. She could see what looked to be bunches of balloons on the terrace and hear the unmistakable hum of a large group of people.

"It looks like there's some sort of private party going on," she said, turning to Lara, but her friend merely grinned.

"Lara, what's going on?" Beverly's heart was beginning to beat a fraction faster, her legs unsteady as she followed Lara along the short winding path.

It was the banner she saw first, the words *Happy Birthday Bev* spelled out in hand-painted blue and green. Below it stood Mark and Deborah, each one beaming, and there was her older sister, who seemed to have brought the whole family along. Her dad was in his wheelchair, a party hat at a jaunty angle on his head, while her mum clutched his hand. School friends were assembled by the bar, while several of her colleagues from the library waved from a table.

They were all here. All here for her.

"Surprise!" Lara cried. Beverly gave her friend a look that said *thank you and I'm going to kill you* all at once. And then they were hugging, and Beverly was crying, and Lara was laughing.

"This wasn't me, you know," her friend confided. "It was all him."

Him.

Taking a deep breath, Beverly wiped her eyes, turned round and walked forward.

Straight into Frank's waiting arms. Ⓜ

Fun In The Sun

The resort was wonderful, the company convivial... if only I could relax and enjoy it

By VIVIEN BROWN

"Wow. Just look at that." John pointed towards the island just starting to come into view below us. "It's beautiful."

I pressed my face against the window as Barbara leaned across us from the aisle seat to get a better look.

"Just look at that gorgeous blue sea," she said, dreamily.

"It really feels like we're on holiday now, doesn't it?" John squeezed my shoulder, almost knocking Barbara's specs off in the process. "And Shelley will be OK without you, Rosie... honestly, she will."

We put our seatbelts on for landing and I told myself he was right. We'd come here to have some fun, a dozen of us from the local tennis club, but unfortunately it was an adults-only trip and that meant leaving my daughter behind.

As teenagers go, Shelley really wasn't too troublesome. Yes, she played her music too loudly and spent far too much time glued to her mobile phone, but I was lucky she and I still got on so well together, especially since the upheaval of the divorce two years earlier. As a teacher, I had seen too many teenagers go a bit wild when things were not going well at home.

With a jolt, the plane touched down, bumping along the Tarmac and bringing my thoughts back down to earth with it.

"Look! Coconut trees!" John was pointing beyond the airport buildings to a row of palms swaying in the breeze, and I couldn't help but laugh. He was always so chirpy, so positive, and although we had agreed to take things slowly, it reminded me why I had grown so fond of him during the short time we had been seeing each other.

Popping my sunglasses on, I followed the others into the aisle and

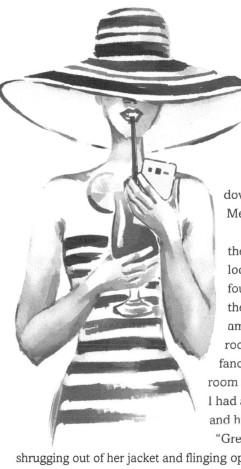

down the steps into the glorious Mediterranean sunshine.

As we all clambered off the transfer coach, the hotel looked impressively grand, its four gold stars twinkling above the door. The married couples among us had booked double rooms but the rest of us hadn't fancied paying exorbitant single room supplements, so Barbara and I had agreed to share, while John and his friend Simon did the same.

"Great view," Barbara said, shrugging out of her jacket and flinging open the doors to the balcony as soon as we reached our room. She delved into her case for a pair of flip-flops. "Shall we unpack now, or go for a wander first? Check out the pool, catch up with the others, maybe see what the bar has to offer…"

A picture of my ex-husband Bill flickered across my mind, and the way holidays used to be. Him off somewhere with his golf clubs, me left alone with a mound of paperbacks and a bottle of Coke – then, after Shelley was born, with a mound of nappies and a bottle of formula milk. I could hardly remember the last time I'd done anything just for me, anything that took me out of the day to day routine I had fallen into during the course of my less than idyllic marriage.   ➜

Joining the beginners class at the tennis club the previous summer had been my first step towards changing all that. I loved it. The exercise, learning the rules, meeting a whole gang of new and interesting people of all ages. In a little over a year, I'd fallen in love with tennis. And, to be honest, I think I had started to fall just a little bit in love with John too. Tall, handsome widower John who had taken me under his wing, asked me out to dinner, and now...

"Do you mind if I stay behind and freshen up a bit first?" I turned away before Barbara wondered what I was grinning at. Thinking about John had that effect on me.

"OK, Rosie. See you later. You shouldn't have any problem tracking us down. And why don't you switch your mobile back on now we're here? Let Shelley know you've arrived safely. I know you want to."

I closed my eyes as a wave of guilt swept over me at leaving her

While most of the others who had chosen to come on the trip were either young and child-free or older couples whose kids had already left home, I was the only one with a teenager, and it had become a bit of a friendly joke among them all just how much I fussed over her.

I watched the screen of my mobile light up, and then there was a short delay as it searched for a local network. Good. There was a strong signal. I waited a few moments, half expecting a text message to arrive, but there was nothing.

Well, no news is good news, I told myself as I sent her a brief *Arrived safely. Love you* text, then stripped off my crumpled travel clothes and stepped under the refreshingly powerful spray of the shower.

The next day was sunny and everyone was sitting around the pool in the afternoon, laughing and chatting, but there had been no text from Shelley, and no call, and it was making me feel uneasy.

I had tried to phone after breakfast, and twice more since lunch, but she didn't answer. Her phone just rang and rang, then switched over to her automated voicemail message. Somehow, hearing her voice telling me she was unavailable and inviting me to leave a message didn't feel right at all. My own daughter had never been unavailable to me before. But then, I'd never left her before either. I closed my eyes as a wave of guilt swept over me.

"Are you coming for a swim?" John was nudging me. "You're starting to burn in the sun, and we can't have you sick before we hit the tennis courts this evening."

"Maybe later. I think I'll pop back up to the room for a while. I'm not used to this heat. Get Barbara to have a dip with you."

I smiled at him and walked away, suddenly realising that I didn't feel the tiniest bit worried about encouraging John to spend time with another woman. Unlike Bill, I trusted him absolutely. I heard Barbara giggle, and then a big splash as he pushed her gently into the water.

L ying on my back on the bed upstairs, listening to the hum of the air conditioning, I tried Shelley's number again. Nothing. She was staying with her father so, of course, I could ring his flat, but it might be Bill himself who answered. I knew that would feel awkward, as though I was checking up, doubting his abilities as a father. If anything was wrong, he would surely let me know.

It crossed my mind, just briefly, that Shelley might be ignoring me on purpose, feeling aggrieved at my going away without her. And with John. I still wasn't really sure how she felt about John.

She'd met him, of course, a couple of times, and they appeared to get on well enough. But I had been treading very carefully, not quite ready to admit that we were anything more than friends, a little afraid of what her reaction might be.

She was only thirteen, and her life had already been pulled apart by a divorce – no matter how amicably done.

"You OK, Rosie?" John whispered when I returned. Everyone had decamped down to the beach and laid their towels out in a row. John had saved me a spot beside him and had bought me a cocktail ➜

with a little umbrella in it, bright yellow to match the parasol fluttering above our heads.

"I'm fine." I wanted him to understand, yet how was I meant to tell him I shouldn't have come? That I should have stayed at home with my daughter? That, much as I cared about him, she had to come first? "It's just that…"

And then, right on cue, my mobile rang, from somewhere deep inside my beach bag. Throwing sun cream and water and tissues out all over the sand, I rummaged desperately for it, grabbing at it before it could stop.

A glance at the screen told me the call was from a number I didn't recognise at all. Oh, please, not an insurance salesman or a shopping survey. I had enough of those at home.

"Hello?"

"Hi, Mum."

"Shelley! Where are you?"

"At Dad's, of course. Where else would I be? Don't tell me you've been worrying?"

"No, of course not," I lied. "Well, maybe just a little. So, what have you been up to without me?"

"Well, Dad took me ice-skating today, and yesterday we went swimming, and then to the cinema. He even made me some veggie paella for tea. Dad in the kitchen! Can you imagine it?" And as she laughed, I could feel all the pent-up stress draining out of my body and seeping away like magic into the sand beneath me. "But how about you and John? Having fun, I hope."

"Oh, yes, it's lovely here. But, Shelley, you've not been answering your phone."

"Sorry about that, Mum, and don't be angry with me, but…" She waited for a moment, as if expecting me to tell her off. "I accidentally dropped it in the deep end at the swimming pool. I know I should have left it in the locker with my clothes. It's completely wrecked. Anyway, Dad bought me this great new one today. It's on a different network, which is why I've got a new number. I suppose I should have used

Dad's phone to call you and say hello, but it's only been two days..."

"So, you're OK?"

"Did you think I wouldn't be? Oh, Mum, stop being such an old worry-guts. You know I miss you, but Dad's not a bad substitute! I want you to enjoy your holiday, not worry about me. You deserve to have some fun in your life...and some romance! But I'll say bye for now. I don't want to use up all the credit on this new phone."

John was looking at me curiously.

"Well? Is she all right?"

"Having a whale of a time, by the sound of it. She's growing up fast, John, and I have to learn to let go, don't I? She's perfectly able to get by without her mother breathing down her neck. And Bill might not have been a great husband, but he's a good dad."

As she laughed, I felt all the pent-up stress drain out of my body

"That's the spirit. And did she say anything about me at all? Did I get the seal of approval yet?"

"Yes, I think you did. She said that I – we – should have a bit of romance in our lives. Oh, John, is it too soon? I know we haven't really talked about the future, but I feel like I've been treading on eggshells, so scared of putting a foot wrong and upsetting her."

"Me too. I wasn't even sure I should peck you on the cheek in front of her! But I'm certainly up for a bit of romance, if you are. Quite a lot of it, in fact!"

"There's nothing I'd like more." I reached for the glass he was holding out towards me and took a sip. "Mmm, lovely. Sex On The Beach! My favourite."

John grinned.

"Perhaps we could go for that swim now, if you fancy it?"

"I'd love to."

I slipped out of my sandals, wiggled my toes in the warm sand and, without a single eggshell underfoot, we walked hand in hand towards the sea. (MW)

On A Sunday Morning

She scoured the brocante for the cup and saucer that would save the life she loved!

By JO THOMAS

Despite the hot, mid-morning sun hitting the wide, plane tree-lined pavements, the air full of the smell of hot coffee and rotisserie-cooked chickens, and the sound of joyful sellers relishing a good morning's work, Cerys was a bag of jangled nerves and in a hurry. The brocante market was in full swing.

All around her couples were walking arm in arm, or calling to each other, pointing to their finds. There was bartering between sellers and buyers for reems of vintage starched fabric, silver cutlery and chairs to be upholstered.

"Non Madame, pas possible!" a seller shook her head as another woman bartered for a pile of linen, before they both agreed a price, nodded, smiled and exchanged euros for goods.

The town square was full of stalls selling all sorts of second-hand goods. In the car park, there were bigger items, dark wooden wardrobes and ornate bedframes laid out on the ground under boughs of the plane trees. The brocante market happened once a month Cerys had discovered. And thank goodness it was here today.

But no one here was in a hurry. Everyone was moving slowly around browsing, picking up items, replacing them, considering them and slowly strolling as if life had just taken it's hand off the tiller for a while and was letting everyone drift on calm waters.

"Excusez moi," said Cerys, quickly scanning the stalls purposefully as she edged through the slow moving Sunday morning shoppers.

She would have loved to have stopped and had coffee, like others were doing, but she didn't have time. She really had to try and find what she was looking for.

Cerys couldn't believe her luck when she'd got the job at the château. Daily life at the call centre had started to take its toll. Sitting day in, day out at the same booth with her head set on, looking at her screen saver of a lavender field in the bright, glorious sunshine.

A scene much like today really. She'd walked from the château ➜

past the lavender fields, breathing in their scent, and more than anything she didn't want to leave, and she didn't want her mistake to be found out.

Cerys had applied for the job after her best friend at the call centre left suddenly, a family bereavement making her realise life was too short not to do the things you wanted to do. She was going to do her bucket list! Cerys didn't have a bucket list. All Cerys had was her screen saver. So when she read an online advert that a château in Provence was looking for waitresses for their wedding season, what did she have to lose?

However, despite passing the skype interview, Cerys had discovered she wasn't that good at waitressing! And yesterday had proved it. Much as she loved the weddings she'd worked on, the actual waitressing part hadn't come that naturally. Helping organise them, talking with the brides and helping make it happen, she had loved.

On the actual day, her track record was fairly disastrous. The time she dropped a knife into the groom's pocket and tried to retrieve it without him noticing... he did! The stacked coffee cups that toppled over into the bridesmaid's lap... And she really couldn't get to grips with that swing door into the kitchen without it always smacking her on the backside!

Now she was at the end of her trial period and tomorrow she had her meeting with the château owner, Juliet. She had to put her most recent mistake right if she was in with a chance of staying on.

She'd been counting out the vintage tea set for afternoon tea for a bridal party arriving on Wednesday. She'd been so careful with them, but then Sebastián, the groundsman, had appeared at the open French doors, making her jump and she dropped the cup and saucer! Now the set was one cup and saucer down and she had to try and find a replacement before Juliet had a chance to notice.

She kept moving past the stalls of fabric, tablecloths, copper pans, kettles and lightshades until finally, she came to what she was looking for. She let out a sigh of relief.

She pulled her baseball cap further down to shield her eyes.

The stall holder, under the shade of the awning, smiled as plates, full dinner services and big patterned serving dishes exchanged hands for euros. Cerys edged in closer to the big boxes of cups and saucers and peered in. All single and looking for a new home. All of them waiting to finally fit in.

She moved around the stall, scouring the second-hand crockery. She saw one cup a little like the one she needed and pulled out the photo on her phone. It wasn't the same. Her spirits started to sag. What on earth was she going to do if she couldn't find a replacement? How was she going to tell Juliet she'd broken something else with her clumsiness? She'd never keep her on past the trial period!

Suddenly, her heart skipped. She spotted a cup out of the corner of her eye, catching the sunlight. Cerys pulled out her phone looking between the two. It was the same cup! Thank

Her clumsiness would ruin her chances of keeping the job!

goodness – and with a saucer! She pushed her phone back into her bag, turned back to the box and reached in, finally letting the sun fill her soul with the warmth of the day.

However, as she pulled out the saucer with one hand, and the cup with the other, it slipped from her fingers. She gasped. She couldn't have dropped another one, could she? But there was no smashing sound. She looked into the box to see another hand on the cup. She glanced up and to her surprise, not only was someone else holding the cup she'd been trying to buy, but it was Sebastian, the groundsman.

"Bonjour," he smiled politely.

"Bonjour," she said, her mouth going dry.

"We seem to have similar taste," he said.

"Um yes…." Cerys said. He smiled at her, a very disarming smile that she couldn't help but return. "I…I was hoping to buy them," Cerys said as calmly as she could.

"Ah, me too," he said tilting his head to one side.

"I really needed them to complete a set," Cerys said urgently. ➛

"Me too," he said, still smiling, but a little more shyly this time. "I wanted them as a gift to someone."

She wondered briefly who he'd be giving them to. But right now, she really needed them.

"I need them to replace a cup and saucer I broke," she said quickly.

"I wanted to give them as a gift to someone who broke a set when I shocked them by coming into the château through the French doors."

Suddenly, Cerys realised what he was saying and began to blush.

"I wanted to apologise and make up for causing her to jump and drop the cup and saucer."

Was she about to be fired and sent away from this placed she loved?

"Ah," Cerys said, "But I need them right away so that my boss doesn't end my trial period tomorrow and I'll have to go home."

"Hmmm, so we have a problem," Sebastian said, making Cerys smile even more. "I tell you what, how about you buy the saucer, and I will buy the cup and we will be joint owners of a cup and saucer, and we can visit them together, in their set?"

Cerys laughed.

"That sounds like an excellent plan, thank you!" she said.

Each of them paid for the saucer and cup separately, much to the stall owner's amusement.

"Now," said Sebastian, "Perhaps, as joint owners, we should go out to lunch so we can get acquainted and reunite our cup with its saucer?" he asked, pointing towards a small bistro down a side street with an awning over a few red and white covered tables. "Henri's bistro does a very good lunch menu," he added.

Cerys hesitated. She should get straight back before Juliet realised the cup and saucer were missing.

"It is lunchtime," said Sebastian, as the church bells rang out for midday. "Everyone in France stops for lunch," he said.

And then with the sun on her face and the smell of herbs and red wine cooking rising up from the little side street, her stomach rumbled, and she smiled. "That would be lovely," she said.

After lunch of soft terrine with tart cornichons and a basket of baguette, rich boeuf bourguignonne in red wine and fragrant herbes de provence, a carafe of chilled wine from the vines in the area, and ice cream for dessert, they finished with small strong coffees.

Cerys put the cup and saucer in her bag and Sebastian drove them back in the château's 2CV, with the roof open, through the lavender fields in the hot summer sunshine.

Cerys finally found herself relaxing and really enjoying herself. The last thing she wanted to do right now was leave.

Back at the chateau, Juliet was waiting for her. "Cerys, there you are. I wondered if we could have our little chat now, instead of tomorrow?"

"Um, yes," said Cerys, suddenly worried she'd taken a two-hour lunchbreak and the cup and saucer were still not back with the others.

Cerys followed Juliet into the cool dining room. Sebastian smiled at her as she went. She wished she could smile back. She loved being joint owner of a cup and saucer with him.

Juliet stood in front of the large dresser where the teacups and saucers were lined up.

"I can explain," Cerys said. "I dropped one yesterday, and I know I seem to do that quite a bit, but look," Cerys reached into her bag and pulled out the cup and then the saucer. "They're the exact match. I took a photograph and found them in the market." She said. "I'm sorry, I broke them, but these are replacements."

Juliet looked at the cup and saucer in surprise.

"Well, that's brilliant," she said. "But actually Cerys, there is something I wanted to talk to you about."

Despite the heat outside in the July sunshine, Cerys felt herself go cold. Was this it? Was she about to get sent home?

"Like you say, your waitressing skills aren't the best," said Juliet.

"No," said Cerys dropping her head.

"But your hard work and organisational skills, attention to detail ➡

and the way you get on so well with the clients is brilliant."

"Thank you," she said, devastated.

"I heard this morning that Rosie, the wedding planner, is planning to leave us, and…" She smiled, "I wondered if you'd like to replace her. Organise the events. It might be safer than having you on waitressing duties!" She laughed.

"Really?" Cerys looked up to check she wasn't joking.

"Absolutely. Who else would get up on their morning off and go and find a replacement cup and saucer? And it's wonderful to finally see you settling into French life and taking some time to relax and enjoy it!" she said with a smile.

"Oh yes! I'd love that!" beamed Cerys.

She looked at the cup and saucer. Perhaps it was time she shared visiting rights with the other owner again – this time with a glass of wine looking over the lavender fields at sunset, to celebrate her new job, a new beginning and finally feeling part of a set where she belonged. (MW)